This novel is dedicated to all the loyal Flash Gordon fans over the years, and to s-f fans like myself who have wanted to escape the bounds of Earth.

# FLASH GORDON:
# MASSACRE IN THE 22nd CENTURY

## tempo
## books
GROSSET & DUNLAP
A Filmways Company
Publishers • New York

# FLASH GORDON: MASSACRE IN THE 22ND CENTURY

# PROLOGUE

The *Aras'Z'Eata,* an 18-million-ton deep space cargo vessel Earthbound from Beta Ceti-IV, came into real space at a catalogued hyper point some eight light years from Sol, and a red telltale began winking on the bridge.

The ship carried bio-chip computer circuits grown on the fourth planet in the Beta Ceti system under conditions that could not be adequately matched anywhere else in the Federation. Despite the frightfully high cost of transportation, the circuits, which were central to any modern computer system, could be distributed by the Trans Fed Company throughout the Federation at an immense profit.

First Officer Alek Romanov, the only man this morning on the bridge, flipped the intercom switch with shaky fingers. "Captain Beluga to the bridge on the double."

A moment later Beluga came on. "What's up, Alek?"

1

"You'd better get up here right away, Stewart," Romanov, a short, swarthy Russian, said.

"I'm on my way," the intercom crackled.

The first officer brought the telltale up on his data terminal, and columns of information began marching across the screen.

Capt. Stewart Beluga shuffled through the bridge port a few moments later, his ever present cup of coffee in hand, and made his way forward between the consoles. "Now what the hell is eating you, Alek?" he grumbled as he slumped down in his acceleration couch and pulled the overhead command module into position.

Romanov started to speak, but Beluga had already noticed the telltale, and he put down his coffee cup and hit the ship's siren and intercom buttons. "Stillman, Heddy, and Bugs, to the bridge on the double," he shouted. Then he flipped the sequence for the ship's computer.

"Guardian," he said softly. For optimum results, ship computers were never to be shouted at.

"Yes, Stewart," a soft, very feminine voice answered, seemingly from a few inches above his head.

"Search and identify the distress signal."

"Can't tell you too much about it, Stewart, except it is an automatic distress signal. Of course, I could give you more information if you released the ship's systems to me."

"You've got them," Beluga said, and there was a long moment of silence while the Guardian did her work.

"There appears to be no Guardian aboard," the computer said and Beluga looked up.

"What?" he said, shocked. No vessel could operate in deep space without some kind of sophisticated computer system to hold it all together.

"The vessel seems to be a primative."

"More data."

"Automatic distress signal. No Guardian. No response on any frequency. Motive drive evidently nuclear."

Beluga snapped forward, his heart hammering. Nuclear drives for intersteller vessels were something only in history books. That type of drive had not been used anywhere in the Federation in more than fifty years, ever since the hyper drive had been invented and intersteller travel had been taken out of the exploration-only stage.

"Is the vessel an exploration ship?"

"She identifies herself as the *Goodhope*. But my data bank has no information on her."

Rupert Stillman, their navigational officer, came on the bridge, yawning, apparently just awakened from a nap. "What's up, Stew?" he asked.

Beluga turned to him. "Distress signal. Looks like an exploration vessel of some kind. A primative. Nuclear drive."

Stillman was suddenly awake, and slipping into his acceleration couch. When he had his module swung in place above his eyes, his fingers played at the control board, and the Guardian began pumping him information.

"We'll match relative velocities," he called to the captain. "Looks like something under 70 percent C."

Thomas Heddy and Hal Bogart—Bugs to everyone aboard—who were the science officer and chief engineer respectively, came on the bridge.

"We're picking up a distress signal. Going in to investigate," Beluga said over his shoulder.

Both men scrambled to their positions, leaving the piloting to Stillman and the Guardian. When they were plugged in, Beluga began snapping orders.

"Tom, see if you can get me an atmospheric from inside."

"Working," Heddy said.

"Bugs, see what you and Guardian can work up for me. Run it up on my auxiliary terminal."

"I'm on it."

Beluga hit a button that raised the forward visiscreen plates, oriented the cameras toward the target, and jammed the magnification control to full on. Hanging ahead of them just under a thousand kilometers and with very little relative motion at this moment was the largest man-made thing any of them had ever seen.

"Guardian," Beluga said.

"Yes, Stewart."

"I'd like some more data on the vessel we're now approaching."

"I'm not getting much from my scanning, Stewart, but as you can see she is very large."

"Specify," Beluga said tersely.

"She is roughly in the shape of the cube 3.1 kilometers on a side, with a mass of just over 98 million metric tons."

Beluga whistled. "Anything new on electromagnetic sweeps?"

"No detectable activity other than the distress signal."

"Life supports?"

"No way of telling for certain, Stewart. Tom is working on it with me, but there is too much shielding. However, from the drain on what we're surmising is a fusion generator, I would say the possibilities for working life support systems are quite high. In the range of 97 percent probability plus."

"Thank you," Beluga said. "Time to target," he snapped.

"Sixty seconds to dock," Stillman called out, his face enclosed in a data screen hood. "I'm showing a spin, so we're coming up on the relative south polar axis. Seems to be some kind of a docking bay, or landing blister."

"Guardian," Beluga said.

"Yes, Stewart."

"Can you detect any gravitational generator activity?"

"None whatsoever. I would guess from her spin that she does not have gravitational generation capabilities."

"Jesus," Beluga said out loud. "What's the probability the vessel is of human origin? Specifically Earth origin."

"Insignificantly less than 100 percent."

"Jesus," Beluga said again.


Since hyper drive had been invented, communications had been a problem as yet unsolved. Radio waves traveled at the speed of light, deep space vessels traveled faster.

Beluga thought about this problem, and what it meant to him at this moment, as he nervously

made his way aft to his tiny cabin from the science
blister forward. He had spent the last two hours in
the observation dome watching his crew's unsuc-
cessful attempts to gain access to the derelict ship.

Short of burning through the hull, it looked as if
there was no way aboard for them.

In his cabin he opened a small floor safe, keyed
only to his fingerprints, and from within drew out
a small bio-chip, which he plugged into a console
above his fold-down desk.

A single red light winked on over the cabin
hatch, indicating that Beluga's cubicle was sealed
from all outside interference, including scanning.

The Guardian's voice came to him from a small
speaker above the desk.

"Trans Federation Directorate circuitry activated. Identify please."

"Stewart Beluga, captain, *Aras'Z'Eata.*"

"Voice prints matching," the Guardian said, and
a moment later: "State your problem, captain."

Beluga took a deep breath, and quickly outlined
everything that had happened to them since the
telltale had shown up on the bridge watch console,
including the fact that his crew had so far not been
able to gain entrance to the massive exploration
vessel now lying dead a thousand meters away
from the *Aras.*

"Advise," he said when he had finished.

"Working," the Guardian said, and Beluga sat
back to wait it out.

Every Trans Fed deep space vessel was equipped
with a Directorate Guardian computer program.
The fact of the program's existence was little
known outside Trans Fed executive circles. Only

Beluga of the crew knew about it. On his death the first mate would be informed, but no others. Both men had sworn loyalty oaths to the Company, as did all executives.

Each time the vessel returned to home base the program was revamped with the latest in company policies and thinking, so that if any problem were to arise while in deep space the computer would make the decision.

"Your instructions are as follows, Captain Beluga," the Guardian spoke, bringing Beluga out of his thoughts. He sat forward. "Number one: Cease all attempts to board the *Goodhope*. Number two: Tow the vessel into Earth orbit. Number three: Special provision, captain's decision; should your vessel be challenged at Pluto Hyper Point by Federation Military Forces, resistance will be optional." Beluga whistled. "Number four: No mention will be made—under any circumstances—to your crew or the Federation military, of this decision. Acknowledge instructions."

Beluga smiled nervously. "Acknowledge," he said, and he withdrew the control from its slot and replaced it in the floor safe.

A confrontation had been building over the past fifteen or twenty years between the Trans Federation computer conglomerate and the Federal government. This now, he thought as he left his cabin, could well be a catalyst to an outright declaration of hostility between the two.

# CHAPTER 1

Past. Present. Future.

Dr. Hans Zarkov, a wizened little old man of eighty-seven, hunched up his coat collar against the windblown rain as he got out of the ground car and hurried with Capt. Alois Drager across the mall to the Federation Military Command Center at Omaha Base.

He felt very much a part of the past at this moment because the sprawling military installation could trace its continuous history back more than four hundred years, long before the Federation had even been thought of. And except for the last five years, much of his life had been spent in the service of various base commanders here.

The present was much changed. Over the past twenty years or so, peace had come to the Federation, and the military had become less of a war-making organization and more of a police force. No longer was oppression widespread on any planet within the Federation.

And the future? Zarkov stopped by the main doors of the administration building and squinted up into the rain at the heavy overcast. The future was up there in the stars. Twenty-five planets in the Federation that stretched a hundred light-years in any direction from Terra of Sol. He could remember when, as a young man, the Federation was nothing more than a world government with satellite colonies on the Earth's moon, Mars, and Jupiter's satellite Ganymede. But fifty years ago, when faster-than-light drive was finally discovered and perfected, the universe had opened up. Suddenly and very dramatically.

"Let's go, doctor," Captain Drager said impatiently as he held the door open.

"Sorry," Zarkov mumbled, and he followed the young military man inside where they passed an identification sentinel unchallenged.

At the end of a long corridor, deserted at this time of the evening, they stepped into a grav tube and were whisked downward several hundred meters into the bowels of Federation Earth Center, where they were met by a brigadier general with an intensely worried look on his face.

"Dr. Hans Zarkov?" the man asked, stepping forward. He was large, broad-shouldered, with a deeply lined face. It looked as if he had not slept in a month, and then with his uniform on.

Zarkov nodded, and shook the general's hand.

"I'm Peter Tesler. I'm so glad you could come on such short notice, doctor." He turned to Zarkov's escort and nodded toward the grav tube. "That will be all, captain."

"Yes, sir," Drager said, and without a word to Zarkov, turned on his heel, entered the grav tube, and was gone.

The general took Zarkov's arm and led him down the corridor. They passed a human sentry and then went through a wide, black opening in the wall that made Zarkov's scalp tingle, and for a moment caused his vision to blank out. The room was being scanned and muted by a highly directed, narrow beam of gravitational energy. Nothing in the electromagnetic spectrum, including light itself, could penetrate.

Three high-ranking military officers and one civilian, who Zarkov immediately recognized as the Secretary of Intersteller Relations, Wilbur Holson, were seated around a narrow conference table that gleamed ebony, each position equipped with a terminal data screen and a keyboard. The four men were in deep discussion.

"Gentlemen," the general escorting Zarkov said, clearing his throat. "He has arrived."

They all looked up, and a moment later the civilian, a man only slightly younger than Zarkov himself, got to his feet. "I hope General Tesler has tendered our apologies for bringing you here like this, doctor."

Zarkov inclined his head slightly. "I've been called to this base on other occasions in a similar manner." The other officers in the room looked as tired and bedraggled as General Tesler, with the same intensely worried expression on their faces.

"I assume by your presence here, Secretary Holson, that this is a matter of some importance," he continued.

The man glanced at the others in the room, and then looked back into Zarkov's eyes. "More important than you can possibly imagine at this moment. If you will just have a seat, we can begin."

Two hours ago Zarkov had been doing scientific research in his laboratory outside Old Salt Lake City on a University of Utah grant, when Captain Drager had arrived with his orders to escort him immediately to Omaha Base. He had not been allowed to inform the University, or even his niece, Dale Arden, nor had the captain been able to tell him what the nature of the summons was, or how long he would be gone, so he took his seat at one side of the table with a certain amount of curiosity. Whatever it was he had been brought here for, it was serious.

Secretary Holson began the meeting. "General Tesler is commander of Federation Station Ganymede. He has been included in this meeting because it was he who escorted the *Aras'Z'Eata* in from Pluto Hyper Point."

The general nodded, and Zarkov forced himself to hold back a dozen questions that had instantly popped into his mind.

Across the table from him was a lieutenant general, apparently in his mid-fifties, who looked more like a Tri-V player than a military commander. Holson introduced him as Gen. Hubert Barnes, commander of Omaha Base.

"He has been and will continue to coordinate our efforts in this matter," Holson said.

"Your predecessor was a close personal friend of mine," Zarkov said pleasantly.

The man smiled wanly. "Before his death he

spoke often of you, doctor."

To Barnes' right was a lieutenant colonel, who
Holson introduced as Alonzo Forte, chief of Sur-
veillance Command, stationed on Base 7 Luna.
And to Zarkov's immediate right was Maj. Gen.
Stewart Redmann, chief of Federation Military
Historical Command.

Zarkov's eyes rose at that, and he leaned that
way. "You wrote the paper recently on com-
parative hyper drive research?"

The man nodded, a faint smile at the corners of
his thin lips.

"Quite brilliant," Zarkov said, now even more
mystified than before. A government cabinet
minister, a base commander, an outpost commander, a surveillance officer, and then an historian. It made no sense.

The data terminal screen in front of Zarkov
blinked on, and he swiveled it toward him as a
computer-traced diagram of some kind of a vessel
filled the screen.

"The Intersteller Exploration ship *Goodhope*,"
the historian, General Redmann, said in a soft
voice.

Zarkov looked up into the intense eyes of the
little man, and then it clicked in his memory and he
looked back at the screen. "She was commissioned
two hundred years ago, 2175 or '76, I believe," the
aging scientist said.

"Actually commissioned 2148," Redmann corrected. "She was completed in 2174, fitted out,
stocked, and finally departed Earth orbit on Octo-
ber 11, 2176. Almost two hundred years ago to the
day."

"And she's back?" Zarkov asked. "Her crew and passengers, or should I say their descendants, with her?"

There was a sudden, ominous silence in the room and Zarkov looked up again from the screen.

"The ship is back," General Tesler blurted. "But her crew and passengers are all dead."

"We don't know that for a fact, Peter," Secretary Holson said sharply.

"You have called me here to help with the investigation?" Zarkov asked quietly.

Holson turned to him and nodded wearily. "You're an expert on early technologies and, frankly, we need your help."

"You'd better tell me the entire story."

"The ship is in a stable orbit 22,000 kilometers out. We've set up a research station just off her south polar axis under the guise of routine quarantine."

"The news media knows she's back?" Zarkov asked.

Holson nodded again tiredly. His hair was snow white and looked almost like the mane of some kind of large animal. "The Director asked for and received a seventy-two hour lid on the newsbreak. But that was twenty-four hours ago."

"Then you'd better be quick with your briefing if I'm to get out there and take a look. As I remember from my history lessons, the *Goodhope* was quite large and impossibly complicated by our present technological standards."

"Roughly three kilometers on a side," the military historian said. "She is the largest moving device ever constructed by any sentient beings. Two

hundred years ago she left Earth orbit with a passenger and crew manifest of 158 men and women.
Her destination, the stars," Redmann continued.
"It was long before hyper drive, so the people
aboard were placed in cryogenic deep sleep, and a
portion of the crew awakened for ten weeks every
ten years."

"It was the only ship of its kind ever to be built,"
Zarkov said.

"Yes," Redmann answered. "At a cost of nearly
1.8 trillion New International Dollars, she nearly
bankrupted the entire Earth's economy."

"Now she's back," Zarkov prompted after a
long silence.

Redmann nodded. "For nearly fifty years the
*Goodhope* continued sending back automatic sig-
nals, but then they stopped. It wasn't until a hundred years later—fifty years ago—when the Federation developed its faster-than-light drive, that a
search was mounted. But it was useless. The dis-
tances were simply too vast, even with computer-
enhanced search patterns. After less than ten years,
the search was given up. The *Goodhope* was officially declared lost."

Holson picked up the story. "Five months ago
the deep space cargo vessel FISS *Aras'Z'Eata,*
Earthbound from Beta Ceti-IV, intercepted an automatic distress signal from the *Goodhope.* Her
prime directive required her to investigate, and
they followed the signal in. There was no response
from on board, other than the distress signal, so
the *Aras* towed her in."

"In hyper drive?" Zarkov asked amazed.

Holson nodded. "Damned near burned up their

drive units because of the load, but the Company wanted the ship. For salvage alone, her worth is nearly inestimable."

"Trans Federation?" Zarkov asked, and Holson nodded. The man looked miserable. The gigantic conglomerate that had its beginnings in the early twentieth century as a computer firm had grown and prospered over the years so that today, in sheer size and budget, it rivaled the Federation government itself.

"Federation Military Command on Ganymede picked up the unusually high mass at Pluto Hyper Point, and General Tesler himself headed the party that went out to investigate," Holson said. He looked at the general, who seemed even more uncomfortable than before.

"When we realized what the *Aras* had in tow, we seized the vessel and brought it to its present Earth orbit," the general said.

He looked frightened, Zarkov thought. He had gone up against Trans Federation and now he was worried. "Now the Company is howling?"

Holson shook his head. "Not a word from them, although they've submitted their salvage claim."

Zarkov's eyebrows rose. "What about the *Goodhope*? What have you found on board?"

"We can't board her," Tesler said miserably.

Zarkov sat forward in his contour chair. "What?"

Tesler was shaking his head. "The hatches are sealed from inside, and we haven't a technician in the service who can operate the *Goodhope*'s ancient mechanisms. I don't think even Trans Fed has the people. I'm sure they figured we'd be calling you and now they're just biding their time until you open her up." The general looked down at his fingernails. "What records we do have are not well documented. For some reason Central Computer is silent on the subject. And we don't want to broach her hull. That's why you were called, doctor. As you can see we're in a bit of a ticklish situation."

"Do you suppose Trans Federation has put a block on Central Computer records?"

"That possibility has occurred to us, doctor," Holson said. Then he shook his head in irritation. "Hell, yes, it's exactly what we think. Trans Fed built the damned Central Computer in the first place. But that in itself is not why we called you. We want you to go up there, get aboard, look the ship over, and find out what the hell happened."

Tesler punched a query into the data terminal in front of him, and Zarkov read the exchange in his own screen.

DISPLAY PRESENT MAJOR DATA
ANOMALIES FOR GOODHOPE SPECS

MAJOR ANOMALIES SEE PREVIOUS
Z7797 THROUGH Z8840

. . . MASS .01 PERCENT ABOVE DESIGN

. . . LARGE STATIONARY BIO MASS IN
VICINITY OF DEEP SLEEP STA

Zarkov looked up from his screen, an odd feeling growing within his gut. "May I?" he asked General Tesler.

The general nodded, and Zarkov queried the computer from his own keyboard.

IS THE .01 PERCENT MASS INCREASE ATTRIBUTABLE TO BIO MASS?

. . . NEGATIVE

CAN INCREASED MASS BE ISOLATED?

. . . VICINITY OF DRIVE UNITS

ANY LIFE SIGNS IN VICINITY OF BIO MASS?

. . . NEGATIVE

IS BIO MASS SUFFICIENT FOR 158 AVERAGE SIZED HUMAN BEINGS?

. . . WITHIN LIMITS

"They're all dead," Tesler said.

"We'll see," Zarkov said absently. He looked up. "I'll have to return to my laboratory for some equipment. And I'd like to bring along an assistant."

Holson smiled. "Colonel Gordon?"

Zarkov nodded.

"By all means, doctor," Holson said.

# CHAPTER 2

Flash Gordon was tired. Every bone in his body ached from being brutally slammed through an anti-gravity pocket, which had the same effect as falling off a twenty-meter ledge.

The trim, good-looking woman crouched on the other side of the featureless room had one V on him; one more and she would be the winner of this match. But he had been finding it difficult to concentrate. She looked too much like his dead wife. And every time she came close, he found his mind spinning back to a much happier time.

A chime sounded somewhere above him, and the woman sprang toward him, her body twisting at just the right moments to avoid the constantly moving pockets of shimmering air that marked the narrow areas of zero gravity.

Flash leapt into the air, using his bare feet against the wall to push himself into the middle of the Tri-V arena, the woman's right foot just catching him in his right armpit. It was a mistake.

Flash kicked out with his left foot, catching the woman behind both knees, the force of his own moving body flipping her over backwards, her body contorting painfully as she encountered a zero-G pocket.

An instant later he was on her, both hands around her tiny neck, his thumbs pressing lightly on the arteries just below her ears.

A chime sounded overhead, and the moderator's voice followed. "V for Colonel Gordon. Score tied at two all. Retire."

Flash got to his feet and reached down to help the young woman up but she contemptuously brushed his hand aside, leapt to her feet, and retired to her own corner.

Tri-V—each V stood for a kill, or a victory—had its origins centuries ago in Earth's ancient Japan. The sport had evolved from jujitsu, Tae Kwon Do, and karate, and only in the last twenty or thirty years had it become a popular amateur event.

The young woman waiting across the arena from Flash was seeded number eighteen on Earth, and moving up rapidly, while Flash, who at one time had been the ranking amateur champion throughout the Federation, had slipped to number eleven.

It was his age, he told his friends. At thirty-six he was no longer as quick as he used to be. But the real reason he was no longer ranked number one was his ruthlessness.

Col. Robert Gordon, Flash since his childhood to all who knew or knew of him, was a Federation Central Intelligence Division agent, and a damned

good one. But eight years ago, when his wife was
brutally murdered, something had seemed to go
out of him. Some edge of softness, even mercy, had
died. He had not become a cruel man, at least not
to good people. But in any kind of competition he
had a tendency to forget himself, to want to win at
all costs. In Tri-V he found himself constantly
holding back lest he hurt someone. He wanted to
keep it at the level of sport, and not deadly competition.

But the woman across the arena from him was
very good, and amazingly quick; he half wondered
to himself, as he waited for the final round to begin, if he could beat her in an all out fight.

Although she was small—standing about a
meter and a half and weighing probably no more
than 50 kilos—her body was lithe beneath the loose
trousers and black belted kimono top she wore.
And in this sport, Flash's nearly two meters, one
hundred kilo frame did not have the advantage.

The chime sounded, and the woman began
cautiously edging away from her corner as Flash
circled slowly to the right.

He feinted a charge at her as he came around a
zero-G pocket, and the woman reacted, kicking
out at him with both feet, her right leg just brushing
the G pocket, flipping her to the floor. Flash sidestepped her left foot, and was behind her, ready for
the kill, but suddenly she deliberately rolled into
the shifting zero-G area and was slammed roughly
out the other side, away from Flash's karate chop
to the neck. He had to reverse stride and leap backwards to avoid her almost instantaneous rush that
sent her slamming against the far wall.

And then time seemed to stretch for Flash as he and the woman continued to feint and parry, much like some kind of strange, convoluted ballet, each of them scoring blows and falls, but with no decisiveness.

It was early evening here in the Los Angeles Rim, and although tonight's matches would not count toward ultimate rankings, they were sanctioned by the Federation Tri-V Association, and thus were well attended. In the outer auditorium the arena event was being holographically projected, although there was no audience participation feedback like in a real match. For this event, as far as the contenders were concerned, they were utterly alone—themselves, without outside interference, pitting their skills against each other.

A sharp blow to Flash's left ear sent him reeling; as he was falling, stunned from the blow, he had to twist to avoid a zero-G pocket, and the young woman was on top of him, her tiny but powerful hands reaching for his throat.

He raised his knee sharply between her legs, but suddenly she flipped over to the side, nearly pulling his leg apart at the knee, and a sharp pain raced through his body.

Tensing every aching muscle, Flash flipped over backwards, carrying the woman with him, both of them slamming into a zero-G pocket that she was not expecting.

Then he was astraddle her on the other side, his powerful hands digging into her throat, and the chime sounded.

"Tri-V, the round to Colonel Gordon," the moderator announced.

The woman beneath him relaxed, and Flash climbed off her, at the last moment impulsively bending down and kissing her lightly on the end of her nose.

"Sweetheart," he said lightly.

A moment later he was flat on his back, the woman's right knee pressing painfully into his groin, her thumbs digging harshly into the sides of his throat. Over the two of them the chimes were warbling, sounding a foul, but the woman did not relent, her teeth bared.

"The vaunted Colonel Gordon losing his life for a kiss," she hissed, but Flash only heard her through a haze, as if she was speaking to him from down a long tunnel.

His ears were roaring and pinpoints of light were bursting in his vision when the dull realization came to him that the woman was actually trying to kill him, and doing a good job of it.

He managed to get his right hand free from the grip of her legs and groping half blindly found her throat and squeezed with his little remaining strength.

The rushing sensation was louder now, and it seemed as though he was floating, but suddenly the pressure was gone, and as he gradually regained his senses he became aware of the warbling chimes, and the young woman slumped on top of him.

Flash eased the woman off him as she started to regain consciousness. The Tri-V arena door opened as he sat up, and two security men and the Association doctor came in. He waved them back, but they hesitated by the door.

"Everything is fine," he said to the men. "She

just got a little carried away."

The three men looked skeptical, but they advanced no farther, and Flash looked down at the young woman lying beside him. Her eyes were open, and she was studying him. She smiled.

"Sorry," she said weakly. "I don't know what got into me. Honestly."

Flash got to his feet and helped the young woman up. "I'd hate to go up against you for real," he said, shaking his head. "Are you sure you're all right?"

"I'm fine," she said, passing a hand over her forehead. "How about you?"

"Battered," he said, and they both laughed.

The three men had withdrawn out of holograph range, and Flash and the young woman turned toward one of the pickups, bowed deeply for the benefit of the audience, and then left the arena hand in hand, brushing past the speechless security men and doctor.

"Miss Behrens, isn't it?" Flash asked the young woman as they made their way down the access corridor to the locker rooms.

She looked up at him. "Melissa to my friends."

He nodded. "You fought well," he said, and hesitated a moment. "Sorry about the kiss—I don't know what got into *me.*"

She laughed, the sound light, almost musical. "To the victor belong the spoils." She looked up into his eyes. "That is, if a kiss was all you wanted."

"Am I being propositioned?" Flash asked, his heart quickening somewhat despite himself.

"Perhaps," she said coyly, drawing close to him.

"I am a good cook. And I could fix us dinner. I have an apartment here in the L.A. Rim."

"Sounds inviting . . ." Flash was about to say, when the arena director came waddling down the corridor in a rush toward them.

"Colonel Gordon," he shouted as he spotted them.

Flash and Melissa parted as the man reached them, out of breath.

"There's a priority call for you in my office. I was told to get you to the phone no matter what you were doing."

A dark expression crossed the young woman's features, but Flash didn't notice. "Excuse me," he said to her. "I'll just be a moment."

She nodded, and Flash followed the arena director back to his office. Zarkov was waiting on the visiphone for him there.

"If there's anything I can do for you, Colonel Gordon, just give a yell," the director said, and he left the office.

Flash sat down at the desk and swiveled the visiphone toward him. Zarkov was calling from his laboratory, and was packing equipment into crates and boxes as he waited for Flash.

"Good evening, doctor," Flash said pleasantly. "Looks like you're getting ready to go somewhere."

Zarkov looked up. "Glad I caught you, Flash. Something has come up and I'm going to need your help for a couple of days." The aging scientist looked haggard.

Flash sat forward. "What is it, doc?" he asked, concerned. Zarkov was almost like a father to him.

"Can't say over the phone, but it's important."
Zarkov put down the box he had been packing on
a cluttered lab table, and walked over to the visiphone. He leaned over his desk, his face nearly filling the tiny screen. "I want you to come here immediately. Tonight. It has already been cleared
with the CID. As of this moment you're officially
assigned to the case with me."

"What's it about?"

"Later," Zarkov snapped uncharacteristically.
"I'll meet you at the Old Salt Lake City private
terminal." He looked at his watch. "Within the
hour?"

"I don't know if I can catch a shuttle that quickly . . ." Flash started to object, but Zarkov inter-
rupted.

"Is the *Intrepid* ready for at least orbital flight?"

Flash's eyes widened slightly and his nostrils
flared, but he nodded. "I'll see you in Old Salt
Lake City within forty-five minutes." He hesitated
a moment. "Should I come armed?"

Zarkov looked at him, and his eyes were bagged
and somewhat bloodshot. "Yes," he said. "And be
careful, Flash," he said. Then he reached out and
switched off.

Flash got slowly to his feet and left the office,
thanking the director waiting outside for the use of
his phone. Then he headed back down to the show-
ers, deep in thought, forgetting for the moment his
date for the evening with his lovely Tri-V oppo-
nent.

Dr. Zarkov had been more than a father to Flash
—he had been an uncle, a friend, an older brother.
Ever since Flash's parents had been killed in a

shuttle explosion on their way to Luna City when Flash was sixteen and was in school at Federation University in Chicago, Zarkov had always been there when needed.

Flash had later gone to the Federation Academy at Colorado Springs, and then had joined the CID, which Zarkov had worked for as a consultant long before Flash was born.

The two of them had been on many assignments together, the most difficult of which had been the trouble on Mars some years back. Zarkov had seemed as worried to Flash this evening on the phone as he had been at that time. And when Zarkov was worried, there was definitely cause for alarm.

When Flash entered the locker room Melissa had already taken her pressure bath, and was air drying herself nude in front of a full-length holomirror.

"Excuse me," he said, preoccupied, and he crossed the room to his locker, where he pulled off his Tri-V uniform and laid out his street clothes.

Melissa had turned around, and she had a fierce expression on her face as he passed her on the way to the baths.

"At least you could have whistled or something," she snapped.

He stopped in mid-stride, somewhat flustered. "Sorry . . ." he stammered. She had a lovely body —trim and muscular without any loss of femininity. She was frankly admiring his nude body.

"Hurry on, Colonel Gordon, and get cleaned up," she said softly. "I've got a couple of bottles of imported off-world wine I'd like to share with you tonight."

"Sorry," Flash said again. "I'll have to take a rain check. Something's come up."

"I won't hear of it," the young woman said over her shoulder as she turned back to the mirror to dry herself.

"Can't help it," Flash said, admiring the curves of her body for a moment longer. "I'll look you up when I get back." He went into the baths, hopped into one of the stalls, and hit a button. As the scented, soapy water mist enveloped his body, he did not hear the young woman, a few minutes later after she had gotten dressed, slamming the locker room door behind her. And within ten minutes he was dressed and headed out himself, all thoughts of the woman gone from his mind.

The *Intrepid* was a five-thousand-ton Federation cutter that from the outside looked like nothing more than a large shuttle boat with a capacity of perhaps twenty-five or thirty troops. Its appearance, however, belied the fact that it was one of the most advanced ships of its kind anywhere in the Federation, with intersteller capabilities as well as great stamina and maneuverability within any type or pressure of atmosphere.

Technically the ship belonged to the Federation on assignment to the CID. But in reality, the ship had been transferred permanently to Flash Gordon's personal account, only being returned once a year to the Federation's retro-fit yard in Berlin for updating to the state of the art.

With Dr. Zarkov's modifications, and work Flash himself had put into the craft, there was nothing anywhere in the Federation that could come close to matching the *Intrepid*'s speed and maneuverability, and only major Federation battle cruisers of the line could match its fire power.

He took a cab to his apartment overlooking the New Los Angeles Inner Sea, packed a few things in a small bag, strapped on his laser pistol, then hurried out to the L.A. Rim Shuttleport just outside of San Bernadino.

The shuttleport was often almost completely deserted at this time of night, and there was no one to see him as he entered the huge hangar and hurried up the ramp into the *Intrepid,* closing the hatch behind him.

He quickly stowed his bag and went to the bridge, where he began flipping switches even before he had strapped himself into the left seat.

As the ship eased off the floor and started slowly forward on its auxiliary anti-grav generator, the huge hangar doors began rumbling open to the night, although the noise of their ponderous movements did not penetrate to the bridge of the ship.

As he cleared the vast opening his radio came alive and a moment later the on-board Guardian activated. "Good evening, Flash. Will you be flying manual or would you like me to program?"

"Old Salt Lake Terminal," Flash said. "Just bring the data up for me; I'll handle it manually."

"Certainly."

"L.A. Rim Tower, this is *Intrepid* FMS Seven-Seven-Seven for atmospheric to Salt Lake City," Flash spoke into the voice pickup above his head.

"Roger *Intrepid,* Guardians matching," the radio crackled.

Lines of data streamed across the bridge terminal screens far faster than any human could read or comprehend, and a moment later the board went green.

Flash hit the automatic thrust sequence and the ship took off nearly straight up, its landing struts retracting and its powerful ground lights winking off. Handling the controls himself, Flash encountered some turbulence between five and fifteen thousand meters, but then he was above it and soaring toward a cruise altitude of just over a hundred thousand meters, where he leveled off, and finally turned over flight sequencing to the Guardian.

He leaned back in his acceleration couch, put his left foot up on the edge of the console, and chewed at his lower lip as he idly watched the Guardian's work streaming across the navigational computer board. Time ... distance ... trajectory to target; three parameters all stacking one within the other in neatly fitting rectangles. No slop. No cross control. No corrective feedback. Nothing but precision. The very best human pilots, and Flash Gordon was near that level, could never hope to match the precision of a Guardian. But on the other hand, no Guardian, even the ones Trans Fed was now building, could match a human being for intuitive reasoning and decision making.

Flash sighed and closed his eyes. Despite Zarkov's urgent phone call, he could not help but think of Melissa Behrens. And yet his thoughts about the young woman were mixed with the remembrances of his wife, Doris.

He had met her a couple of years before the Martian trouble had popped up, when she was working as a CID clerk in Surveillance. She was bright, pretty, and very much alive. They had taken old-fashioned picnics together, had gone wind sailing for five days in the South Pacific, and when Dr. Zarkov's brother, a man almost like an uncle to Flash, had died, she had been at Flash's side helping him through the ordeal.

A short three months after they met, they were married and settled down in an apartment on Lake Michigan near the Federation University.

For two glorious years they had led an idyllic existence that was shattered suddenly when Flash was assigned to break up a suspected smuggling ring bringing hypno-gems in from Mizar, very near the edge of the Federation.

He had been warned, in a blanked out visiscreen call the evening before he left, that repercussions would occur should he attempt to rendezvous with the trader ship coming in with the gems as it approached earth, inside Lunar orbit. He had headed out anyway.

As he was lifting off the ramp from the deep space port outside Chicago, he received a frantic call from his wife, but was cut off a moment later. He aborted the mission for the time being, but by the time he had made it back to his apartment, his wife was dead. She had been brutally beaten to death.

Flash had gone out to the rendezvous then with revenge in his heart, and when it was over seven men were dead, the smuggling ring was beaten, and the hypno-gems were destroyed. His wife's murderers were never found.

From that moment on, Flash had never been the same. Nor, he supposed, would he ever be.

The navigation board chimed, and the Guardian's voice came to him, soft and feminine. "Shall I take her in, or would you like manual control?"

"Take her in," Flash said absently as a combination of Melissa Behrens' and his wife's face swam into his mind's eye, his gut tightening.

After his wife's death, the trouble had come up on Mars and Flash and Zarkov had gone to help straighten things out. Zarkov's niece, Dale Arden, had come along with them, and she had fallen head over heels in love with Flash.

Looking up now, out of his thoughts, he supposed that he had leaned on Dale during those dark days, and she had taken his actions as a sign that he was reciprocating her feelings when in reality he was lost, and did not really know what he was doing or where he was going.

But that was nearly eight years ago. Since that time Flash had thrown himself into his work, which on occasion brought him and Zarkov together, and of necessity, Dale Arden. She had become the one woman, other than his wife, for whom he did not have to play any roles. With Dale he could be himself; nothing more or nothing less.

The *Intrepid* came heavily through a layer of clear air turbulence over the Old Salt Lake City Shuttleport, but then settled in crisply for a perfect landing, and Flash took over the ground controls, taxiing to the private terminal at the west side of the port.

When the engines were shut down, he brought up the bridge lights, opened the port, and hurried down the ramp into the cool evening air.

The private terminal seemed deserted, the main building dark about a hundred meters across the parking ramp from the *Intrepid*. Flash had just started that way when, about twenty meters from his ship, a bright flash from the shadows at one side of the building disintegrated a ten centimeter section of plasti-cement next to his feet. Someone was shooting at him.

Flash dove to the left, rolling twice as two more shots were fired at him, each nearly finding their mark, and then he was on his feet, laser pistol in hand, running and dodging toward the shadows on the opposite side of the terminal building.

A laser flash from the corner of the building opposite him hit wide of the mark, and Flash snapped off two quick shots in that direction, the ozone rich in the air. Then he was around the edge of the building where he pulled up short, his heart racing, but there was a thin smile on his lips.

Zarkov had hinted at trouble, and possibly some danger, but Flash had not suspected it would be starting so soon. He only hoped that Zarkov and Dale were all right.

He peeked around the corner of the building in time to see two men, pistols in hand, racing his way. In one quick motion he stepped around the corner as he slipped down into a crouch and brought his weapon up.

Both men saw him at the same time, and started to aim their weapons, but Flash quickly fired two shots, hitting both men in the center of the chest, and they were down.

For several moments, Flash remained crouched at the corner of the building, waiting for someone else to show up, but the night was still, and he finally straightened up and cautiously approached the men sprawled on their backs.

Both of them were dead, holes burned neatly through their chests. Flash holstered his pistol and quickly went through the dead men's pockets, the bile rising up from his stomach. He found identification plates on both bodies, and he did not have to hold the cards up to the light to know that they were Federation Central Intelligence Division IDs.

He studied both men's faces. He had never seen either of them before, but that meant nothing. The CID was a large organization spread over two dozen planetary systems. Yet looking down at the two men, Flash was nearly certain they were imposters—that they weren't really from the CID. But who they were, and why they wanted him dead, he hoped Dr. Zarkov could tell him.

# CHAPTER 3

Zarkov's ground car was just pulling into the parking lot when Flash Gordon came around the side of the terminal building, and relief washed through him like a cool wind on a hot summer's day.

A dozen black thoughts had run through his mind, among them a vision of his old friend's body lying somewhere nearby. The two men had been waiting, and had Zarkov arrived first there was no doubt in Flash's mind that they would have killed him.

He headed across the parking lot as the ground car whined to a halt; it settled to the pavement and its headlights went off. A moment later Dale Arden was jumping from the driver's side and shouting his name; she rushed across to Flash and threw her arms around his neck.

"What are you doing here?" he asked as she clung tightly to him.

Over her shoulder he could see Dr. Zarkov climbing wearily out of the car, and when the old man caught Flash's eye he sighed deeply and shook his head.

Dale, who was tall, somewhat on the thin side, with long, flaming red hair, released her grip on Flash and stepped back to look up into his eyes, a pout forming on her lips. "Some greeting," she snapped, and then she smiled brightly. "When Uncle Hans told me that you and he were going to be working together again I signed on as an assistant."

Zarkov had come up to them, and Flash shook his head. "Not this time, Dale," Flash said. "You can take the car back home."

She started to object, but something in Flash's expression caused Zarkov to interrupt.

"What is it, Flash? Trouble already?"

Flash nodded grimly, and glanced across the empty parking lot toward the terminal access road. "Two men were waiting for me when I landed. They were carrying CID identification."

Dale's eyes widened and she looked past Flash at the shadows around the edge of the building. "Where are they?" she asked. She looked back up at Flash. "What happened?"

"What's happening is that you're going home, and your uncle and I are getting out of here. Now!"

"Not without me!" Dale snapped, and she turned to Zarkov. "Tell him, Uncle Hans."

Zarkov looked plainly worried, but again he shook his head. "It's already been cleared. She can help."

Flash was angry, and he grabbed Dale by the shoulders and looked directly into her dark, brown eyes. "Look, kid, two men have already been killed, and if I had shown up five minutes later they would have murdered you and your uncle."

"I'm no kid!" Dale snapped, and she pulled away from Flash's grasp, went back to the ground car and began pulling out boxes of equipment from the back seat.

"They could not have been CID people," Zarkov said, his voice low and urgent.

"I didn't think so," Flash said, watching Dale angrily working. "But who? And what's this all about?"

"I'm sure they're Trans Federation people, but I didn't think they'd do anything like this so soon." Zarkov looked haggard. "I'll explain everything to you as soon as we get out of here."

Flash nodded. "You can't convince Dale to return home?"

Zarkov managed a grim smile. "She just finished a paper on computer psychology. Best in the field. We can use her."

"I hope she doesn't get in the way," Flash said, but a part of him was secretly glad she was coming along.

Within ten minutes they had stowed the half dozen cases of equipment Zarkov had brought with him in the *Intrepid*'s after storage compartments, had indexed the hull integrity, and had taken off, navigating on a course-chip the aging scientist had brought with him.

Flash was in the left seat, watching the data march across the nav terminal; Zarkov was in the right seat feeding the Guardian computer data on the *Goodhope* he had brought with him; and Dale, still angry, was strapped in an acceleration couch behind them.

As they rounded the hump, five hundred kilometers above the coast of Australia, Zarkov placed a closed circuit call to Omaha Base. He explained what had happened at the shuttleport terminal to an anxious General Barnes, who agreed to take care of everything Earthside.

"Have you explained the situation to Colonel Gordon yet?" the general in charge of the operation asked.

"I'm going to do that right now," Zarkov said. "But I think this pretty well proves Trans Federation's intentions."

"Yes," the general said bitterly. He turned away from the camera and said something to someone off-screen, then turned back. "There's not a damned thing we can do about it either. Not yet, anyway. Not until we have concrete proof. Secretary Holson is still here with me, and he asks that you be particularly careful. Trans Fed has sent a surveillance team up there just to keep an eye on what they're calling 'their investment.' If there's any trouble openly with Trans Federation people, we could be in a big jam."

Flash flipped a switch so that the call came over his console as well, splitting the image at General Barnes' phone.

"Can you tell me what this is all about, general?" he asked.

Barnes looked startled. "I'll leave the explanations to Dr. Zarkov, colonel. But my instructions to him go for you as well. Be careful. We can't step on any toes at this point."

"Why?" Flash snapped. Politics was not, nor had it ever been, his game.

"Because those are your orders, *colonel*," the general barked, accenting Flash's rank. "At this point Trans Fed has a legitimate claim on the *Goodhope*. We're merely up there to find out what the hell happened."

Flash heard a perverse chuckle from the seat behind him, but he ignored it. "Yes, sir," he said crisply to the general, then reached out and flipped off his screen.

A few moments later Zarkov terminated the call, studied the navigation board a moment, then swiveled in his seat to face Flash.

"We've got a few minutes yet before we dock with the *Goodhope,* so I'll go over this quickly. Later you can study the tapes I've brought with me. I've also dug out the *Goodhope*'s schematics from Central Historical Data Bank, although there wasn't much there."

"I assume the *Goodhope* is a ship of some type. A ship that Trans Fed has laid a claim to."

Zarkov was nodding. "It is . . . or should I say *was* . . . an exploration vessel that left Earth orbit two hundred years ago."

Flash whistled, and reflexively glanced out the forward port screen, which had automatically darkened almost opaque as the ship faced into the harsh glare of the sun. "It must have had nuclear drive. No gravitational generators. No Guardian system. Cryogenic deep sleep."

"Right on all counts, Flash."

"And now she's back. How about her crew and passengers?"

"A Trans Federation cargo vessel picked up her automatic distress signal five months ago on the return Beta Ceti run. The crew set up an approach and tried to contact the vessel, but there was no response. When they realized she was a primitive, with apparently no one alive or awake on board, they took her in tow."

"Ganymede Station probably picked them up at Pluto Hyper Point, seized the vessel, and brought her into an Earth orbit under quarantine."

"Exactly. And now Trans Federation wants her back."

"Why?" Flash asked puzzled. "I would have thought they would have merely billed the Federation for towing costs. They could have made a hell of a lot more money that way than bothering with salvage rights. And why try to kill me?"

"You don't understand," Zarkov said.

"The atomics can't be worth much. And unless the ship holds cargo . . ." Flash trailed off because of the odd expression on Zarkov's face.

"Salvage, Flash," Zarkov said softly. "Scrap metal."

"That's ridiculous," Flash said.

"Not when it involves a ship a bit more than three kilometers on a side, with a mass of nearly a hundred million metric tons."

Flash stared at his aging mentor for several long moments until he realized his mouth was hanging open. "My God," he breathed. Then he shook his head. "How about the crew and passengers?"

"One hundred and fifty-eight of them started out on the mission two hundred years ago. Scanning shows a bio mass that is within limits for that number of people in the vicinity of the deep sleep stations."

"Then the question of ownership is meaningless as far as Trans Fed is concerned. The crew and passengers own her, if she was set up like any other exploration vessel. A government builds her and, never expecting the ship to return, it deeds the vessel and everything on board to the crew and passengers."

"It's very likely all hands are dead," Zarkov said.

"Very likely?" Flash asked, a cold chill passing up his spine.

"No one can get aboard. Which is why I was called up. I was told there isn't a technician in the Federation who can troubleshoot anything so mechanically and electronically complex as the *Goodhope*. Ever since biotronics and magnetronics became the way of life, electronics has been a lost art. It would be like the technicians aboard the *Goodhope*, trained to fix an electronic system, trying to make a decent Stone Age ax. A lot of rocks would be ruined before they'd figure it out. If ever."

"And why was I called in on this?" Flash asked straight-faced. He knew what the answer would be.

"Two reasons," Zarkov said, sighing deeply. "The first is that I knew Trans Federation would give us trouble. And the second . . ." He hesitated a moment. "The second reason is nothing more than a visceral instinct. A hunch based on an anomaly."

Flash said nothing, waiting for the old man, who at this moment seemed older and more tired than Flash had ever seen him, to continue.

"A .01 percent mass increase over the *Goodhope*'s design has shown up. Sensors indicate the excess weight is centered in the vicinity of the drive units."

"Trans Fed has been aboard already. Somehow. They're playing some kind of a game with us," Flash said thoughtfully.

Dale had sat forward, and she broke in now. "Either that or sometime during the past two hundred years the *Goodhope* made a planetfall and took on the extra mass."

Flash turned in his seat to look back at her. If that indeed was the case, he thought, did it have anything to do with the likelihood that the passengers and crew were now dead?

A proximity warning sensor chimed on the console and Flash turned to flip it off, but his hand wavered over the button for a long moment as he stared, once again gape-mouthed, at the sight out the forward view screens.

A huge ship, if it could be called that, obviously man-made, hung against the harsh backdrop of stars directly ahead of them. As it slowly spun, the harsh glare of sunlight flashed brilliantly off a million different planes and angles, lending a diamondlike appearance to the thing. The sight was at once awesome and beautiful.

Flash hit the button silencing the warning sensor, and opened the military communications channel.

"This is the FMS *Intrepid* on a docking course for the *Goodhope.*"

"That's a roger, *Intrepid*. Open a Guardian channel and let them match."

Flash flipped the appropriate switch on his command module, allowing direct interface with his on-board Guardian computer and that of the military command post that had been set up in the quarantine module standing off the *Goodhope*'s sunside flank.

"Is Dr. Zarkov with you?" the radio blared.

Zarkov reached up and switched on his own communicator. "This is Zarkov."

"Good morning, doctor," the radio crackled. "My orders are to offer you any assistance you may need, or stand off if that is your desire."

"Has there been any change in status?"

"Negative. We've done nothing more than scan for life forms, and shunt off the distress signal so it doesn't make a mess out of routine nav channels."

"Have your people stand off then . . ." Zarkov started, but his signal was overridden with another.

"FMS *Intrepid,* this is Trans Federation Executive Delta-Hotel-Echo, requesting permission to send one man with you."

Flash reached angrily for his communications channel, but Zarkov silently waved him off.

"Trans Federation Executive, this is Dr. Hans Zarkov. We'd be happy to have one of your people along with us."

"We're happy you are taking that position, doctor. We'll rendezvous with you immediately."

"I assume by that action you will be taking full responsibility for systems integrity should we find any survivors aboard."

"We don't understand, doctor. What do you mean?"

"I mean simply, Trans Federation Executive, that if something should go wrong and life support integrity should be lost, you will take full responsibility for loss of life."

"No life forms are indicated."

"Perhaps," Zarkov said with a slight smile. "Nevertheless I must insist, for the record, that Trans Federation take full responsibility."

There was a silence for several long seconds, but then the Company spokesman was back on the channel. "Trans Federation will stand off, doctor, but we will monitor, so alert your sensory equipment for the intrusion."

Zarkov reached out and flipped off the communicator. "Bastards," he said half under his breath.

It was the first time Flash had ever heard his friend swear. He was amazed. Zarkov had always been a patient, kindly man, who seldom if ever had bad words for anyone. To hear him now like this was strange.

"One hundred and fifty-eight men and women— babies actually; when they left they were all in their early to mid-twenties—are over there, probably dead, and the Trans Federation vultures want only to protect their salvage rights," Zarkov said, his voice filled with emotion. He turned to look out the forward screen, which was now completely filled with the *Goodhope's* bulk. "One of man's first efforts toward the stars. My God, sending that ship out to the stars was like sending an ancient wind sailing vessel to Mars. Their chances of success were the same. Nearly zero. This ship belongs in a museum. It should be a shrine. Not salvage."

"Guardian," Flash said softly.

"Yes, Flash," the computer answered.

"I'm releasing the navigational chip and taking manual control for immediate docking with the south polar axis of the vessel dead ahead. I want you to begin scanning that vessel, and all approaches out to at least a hundred kilometers." As Flash spoke his fingers played over the control board and command module, releasing the automatic navigational control to manual, and matching relative velocities. At this point he did not have to worry about matching spin, because they would be docking at a point along the *Goodhope*'s tremendous bulk that was spinning on its own axis, and therefore stationary.

The *Intrepid* began moving slowly across the forward face of the huge ship, various ports, screens, vents and other protrubances sliding past their forward view screens, all of it scarred and blackened from deep space travel.

Without being specifically asked, the Guardian computer had set up the routine navigation problem on the nav terminal, based on relative velocity data and *Goodhope* information it had received from Dr. Zarkov's chips. The south polar axis was represented simply by a target with an expanding circle at the center representing the relative size of the actual docking area, and a pair of cross hairs representing the deep space lock on the port side of the *Intrepid*. Flash merely had to fly the diagram, matching the cross hairs with the circle at the center of the three-dimensional target.

"Have we got an accurate atmospheric for the *Goodhope?*"

"Ninety-eight percent Earth normal," the Guardian said softly. "It's a little rich in oxygen, but quite breathable."

"We'll be wearing our suits in, Guardian, and I want you to feed us scanning information as you receive it. If any systems aboard the *Goodhope* should change status, I want to be immediately notified. Likewise, if any vessel approaches within the one hundred kilometer range, I want to be informed."

"Will do," the Guardian said.

The *Intrepid* slipped past the lower edge of the *Goodhope,* the Earth, blue and white beyond it, suddenly coming into view, and the south polar axis port, which was a huge curved door in the side of a blister hanging out from the vessel's hull lying dead ahead. And then they were beneath the huge ship, its bulk slipping overhead, as Flash carefully maneuvered his ship toward the polar axis port, exactly matching the relative velocities with a fine touch on the controls, until they were stopped dead in relationship to the port, which lay less than twenty meters off the *Intrepid's* deep space hatch.

Flash hit the automatic systems switch and as he climbed out of his acceleration couch he looked up. "Keep us at this relative position, Guardian."

"Holding," the Guardian said calmly.

He turned back and helped Zarkov out of the acceleration couch, and together with Dale they worked their way aft to the *Intrepid's* staging room and deep space hatch access area. It was the largest

uncluttered area anywhere aboard the ship. The
three of them had plenty of room to stand upright,
stretch, and then pull on their pressure suits, checking each others seals.

Zarkov turned and began pulling the boxes he
had brought with him out of the storage compartments, finally selecting a metal case with a handle,
much like an old-fashioned suitcase. He brought it
over to a low equipment rack, laid it on top, and
opened it. Inside the case, cushioned in slotted
cutouts in some kind of soft, spongy material, were
several dozen instruments, none of which Flash immediately recognized.

Standing next to Zarkov he reached out and
picked up one of the devices, which consisted of a
long narrow blade with a round handle attached at
one end.

"A screwdriver," Zarkov said with a half smile
on his face. "The *Goodhope* was constructed before
the days of keyed molecular bonding. Access
plates, equipment components, in fact a whole host
of various things—the list would be endless—were
loosely bonded with tiny, threaded rods. At the end
of these fasterners is a narrrow slot that matches
the blade of the screwdriver."

Flash studied the highly polished museum piece
a moment longer, then laid it carefully back into
the case, and Zarkov closed the lid and latched it
lovingly. "I designed and built these tools a few
years back from specifications in old paper books
and manuals."

He looked up at Flash. "With any luck these
tools should be the key to getting us aboard the
*Goodhope.*"

"Then what?" Flash asked.

Zarkov looked at his niece. "I wish you would remain here, my dear."

Dale had her pressure suit helmet down from its locker and she looked at her uncle and then Flash, and shook her head. "I don't want to be left behind, Uncle Hans," she said, and she put her helmet on, sealed it, and an instant later her suit functions whined on.

Zarkov turned back to Flash. "I've put the *Goodhope* chips I brought with me into the Guardian's data bank. She'll be able to guide us to the deep sleep station. It's near the center of the ship. I want to determine what killed the crew and passengers. We may be able to key into the ship's data bank, if she has one, for more information."

"And then the drive units?" Flash asked.

Zarkov nodded. "Before we release the ship to Trans Federation we've got to find out what caused the increase in mass. At .01 percent we're talking about nearly ten thousand metric tons. That's twice the size of the *Intrepid*."

Flash pulled down Zarkov's helmet and helped his friend with it, then pulled on his own helmet, the suit functions coming immediately to life as the seals were made, the status indicators inside his face plate winking green.

"Guardian," he said.

"I'm with you," a soft voice said inside his helmet. "The status aboard the *Goodhope* remains the same except in the vicinity of what is the control center. There is a low power drain to some kind of an indicating circuit."

Flash looked up. "What's the probability the indicating circuit is some kind of a proximity detector sensing our presence?"

"Hard to tell for certain, Flash," the Guardian said, sounding almost thoughtful. "But I would say in excess of 80 percent."

The ship, at least, was still alive, Flash thought. "Intruders?"

"None," Guardian said.

"Keep me advised."

"Certainly."

"Dale?" Flash said looking over at her.

She nodded, her helmet moving ponderously. "I read you."

"Dr. Zarkov?" he said.

"Let's go."

Flash moved to the hatch, hit the button, and the huge door slid silently open. The three of them crowded inside the airlock. Dr. Zarkov clutched the tool kit as Flash closed the inner door, cycled the air out, and opened the outer hatch, a tiny puff of ice crystals falling like snowflakes.

The *Goodhope*'s landing blister, less than twenty meters away, was huge—large enough if the doors were opened to simultaneously accommodate a dozen ships the size of the *Intrepid*.

Zarkov pointed to an area to the right of the huge port doors. "Looks like an airlock hatch," his voice came over the suit radio. "Let's try there."

The three of them kicked away from the *Intrepid,* one at a time, and a few seconds later were standing on a small metal-runged porch at the level of what obviously was an airlock.

Zarkov snapped the tool kit against the hull of the ship, then with his helmet light on, began searching the area to the right of the door seam, immediately finding a small access plate, held in position with three recessed screws.

He opened the tool kit, withdrew one of the several screwdrivers, and quickly removed the three screws, the plate popping open on its hinges.

In a shallow recess behind the plate were dozens of wires, several indicator lights now glowing green, and two large terminal blocks.

"Guardian," Zarkov's voice came over Flash's suit radio.

"Yes, Dr. Zarkov."

"Would you search the *Goodhope* data I gave you for airlock schematics?"

"Working," the Guardian said, and a moment later she was back. "Need more data, Dr. Zarkov. The airlocks seem to be indexed with a seven digit number."

Zarkov peered closer into the recess behind the service plate, but it was Dale who found the number stenciled above the airlock. She called it out to the Guardian.

An instant later a complicated schematic diagram flashed onto their helmet screens, and Zarkov studied it for several long minutes, finally grunting his satisfaction. From the tool kit he withdrew a short probe with a wire attached to it. At the opposite end of the wire was a tiny, springed clip. Carefully Zarkov clipped the wire to one terminal and then standing back slightly, touched the probe to another contact on the second block, and the airlock door ponderously opened on its massive hinges.

# CHAPTER 4

Flash reached up and flipped on his pressure suit's external audio pickup and held his breath, listening for a sound, any sound, but all was silence aboard the *Goodhope*. It was an ominous silence that made him feel uncomfortable. It was the silence of a tomb.

They stood just inside the airlock on what obviously was a hangar deck. Dim lights far overhead lent a soft glow to four large vessels that appeared to be shuttle craft, lined up in their racks all facing the huge, curved doors. Flash took a step toward them.

They had never been used. It was clear from the still unblemished nose cones and hulls of the escape ships. Which meant that the *Goodhope*'s crew had never made planetfall. At least not in their own shuttle craft.

"It's sorta' spooky," Dale's timorous voice came over Flash's suit radio, and he turned toward her.

She stood a few meters in from the airlock they had just entered. Zarkov was peering at some kind of instruction plate next to a panel of controls and lights. After a moment the aging scientist looked up and turned back toward Flash.

"This was designed to be used as an emergency escape hatch, which is why there were no controls on the outside of the ship," he said.

"How did they get in and out of here routinely, then?" Flash asked, and he could almost hear Zarkov shrug.

"The shuttle craft, I suppose. But I imagine there must be maintenance airlocks all along the hull. The schematics I brought along show hundreds of airlock systems."

"Is there any way of telling whether or not this airlock was ever used?"

"Not from here," Zarkov said. "But if there's a central data bank, some kind of on-board computer system, it would probably know." He half turned to look at the airlock again. Above it was stenciled the word EMERGENCY with the airlock number below it.

"Guardian, can you read me?" Flash said.

"I'm reading you, Flash. There is some kind of interference, however, that I cannot localize. I'm trying to filter it."

Zarkov had turned back again from his study of the airlock. "Has there been any change in the *Goodhope*'s status?"

"There was a brief indicator drain in the control room near the outer hull, which is about two kilometers from your present position. I am assigning an 80 percent plus probability that it indicated the cycling of the airlock you activated."

"Any change in the status of the bio mass?" Dale asked, and Flash could hear the hopefulness in her voice.

"I'm afraid not, Dale," the Guardian said pleasantly. The computer recognized Dale from previously recorded voiceprints. "There has been no change in status."

"Localize the deep sleep area and bring up the proper corridor diagram on my suit screen," Flash said.

"Working," the Guardian replied, and a moment later images began streaming across the tiny visiscreen above the face plate in Flash's helmet, finally slowing and stopping at a complicated diagram.

"Simplify please," Flash said. "And localize our position."

The image on Flash's visiscreen seemed to clear, and a tiny red dot began winking at a wide area in the bottom center of the diagram. An even larger open area directly above them was outlined in bright green.

He studied the diagram for a long moment, then turned again to Dale. "I'm going to ask you one more time, Dale, to return to the *Intrepid* and wait for us there. You can work with Guardian from the data we're sending back."

"No," she said.

Flash sighed deeply, then looked toward Zarkov. "Let's get this over with then," he said, and he turned and trudged across the hangar deck in a curious, stiff-legged gait. Here at center of the ship, where there was no spin, they were in an area of weightlessness. At the ship's hull, the farthest from the axis of spin, gravity was probably near Earth normal.

The diagram in Flash's visiscreen indicated a shaft running straight up the ship's axis, with an opening at the rear of the hangar deck. Just behind the shuttle craft, he found the opening and peered inside. Red lights shown at what were apparently deck openings, gleaming off the metal surface of the wide tube; the lights fading and finally being lost to the distance three kilometers straight up. Handholds had been placed at frequent intervals as far as Flash could see, but before he started up he studied the diagram a moment longer. The deep sleep area appeared to be located a dozen meters off this shaft along a main corridor that bisected the huge ship, which meant it was around one and a half kilometers straight up from where they stood now.

"Ready?" he asked, turning back to Zarkov and Dale.

"After you," Dale said, and Zarkov nodded.

Flash ducked into the shaft, released his suit's sole plates from the deck, and kicked off, gracefully moving straight up the shaft, pulling himself along with the handholds.

Looking down after he had passed the first few deck openings, he could see Dale's suit lights about ten meters below him, and the same distance below her, Zarkov was bringing up the rear.

As he continued up the shaft, hand over hand, the *Intrepid*'s Guardian computer traced their progress, showing their position as a red dot moving up the axis shaft toward the main corridor intersection.

About halfway to the intersection, the Guardian

came on, faint, and over some static. "Flash, are
you reading me?"

"Yes, but your signal is breaking up."

"There is an intrusion on my systems," the
Guardian said, and although it was theoretically
impossible for a computer, even one so sophisticated as a Guardian, to show emotion, Flash was
certain he could detect a note of concern in her
voice.

"What kind of intrusion," he asked, missing a
handhold, and drifting slowly upward.

"I don't know," the computer voice said. "It
seems as if I am being monitored. But I cannot localize the point of contact."

"Did you catch that, Dr. Zarkov?" Flash asked,
looking down the shaft. Dale and Zarkov had
fallen farther behind, but were now slowly catching
up.

"Yes, I did," Zarkov said, obviously out of
breath. "Guardian, where is the Trans Federation
Executive vessel at this moment?"

There was a silence as Flash continued to drift
slowly up the shaft. When the Guardian computer
returned, Flash was sure he could hear a new note
of uncertainty.

"I cannot accurately sense the Trans Federation
vessel, but my proximity detectors show an area of
gravitational anomaly at the ship's last position."

"Please excuse the intrusion, Dr. Zarkov," another voice, this one much stronger and with no
interference, blared in their suit radios.

"Trans Federation," Zarkov said. "I'd like to
see the bio circuitry you are using for this neat little
trick."

"It's quite new, doctor, but we would be happy to let you look it over once you finish aboard the *Goodhope.*"

"Guardian," Flash said softly.

"Yes, Flash," the computer answered.

"I want you to immediately block out all sensory data from the *Goodhope,* and break off communications with us."

After a moment of silence, the Guardian was back. "I can't do that, Flash. I no longer have control over much of my compliance circuitry."

"Please continue your search, Dr. Zarkov, Colonel Gordon, and Miss Arden. We mean you no harm. We wish nothing more than to accurately monitor whatever you may find."

"Then release our Guardian. We need her data bank and correlative functions," Zarkov said calmly. He was stopped just a few meters below Flash and Dale.

"I'm sorry, we cannot do that, doctor," the Trans Fed spokesman said smoothly. "But we will relay to you anything you may need. In fact, we're setting it up at this moment so that you can have an apparent direct contact with your machine. Please continue."

Zarkov looked up past Dale at Flash and shook his head helplessly. After a moment Flash looked up the shaft, then at the image still on his visiscreen. They were here to do a job and, with or without Trans Federation interference, they were going to finish it. But as Flash started up the shaft it was with the grim determination that once they had finished here he was going to pay a visit to the Trans Federation vessel. A visit that Trans Fed would remember for a very long time, despite General Barnes' orders to the contrary.

Within ten minutes they had gone the remaining distance, and Flash stepped out of the shaft into a wide corridor that curved uphill toward the area of increasing gravity a kilometer and a half away at the hull.

He helped Dale and then Dr. Zarkov out of the axis shaft, and, once again checking the simplified ship's diagram on his visiscreen, Flash led them down the corridor to a large, white door that looked very much like an airlock. Above it, the words CRYO SLEEP STATION were stenciled in bold red letters. Beside the door, at chest height, was a panel with a single large button, glowing softly green. The corridor was well-lit and seemed immaculately clean, although old-fashioned, with visible overlapping seams in the walls, and pipes, wires, and grilles seemingly covering every square centimeter of space other than the floor itself, which was a soft plastic.

"Guardian," Zarkov said.

"Yes, Dr. Zarkov."

"Can you localize an atmospheric for me in the deep sleep station itself?"

"Negative," the Guardian said, "but I am showing some kind of sensory equipment for the deep sleep station, with read out equipment in your immediate vicinity."

"Have you got that wiring diagram?"

"Working," the Guardian said, and then a few seconds later: "Negative."

"Stand back, Dale," Flash said, and he reached out and hit the button.

The massive door slid smoothly apart in four triangular wedges that recessed into the overhead bulkheads and into the floor, revealing a large, dark room. As they stood on the threshold, the room lights slowly began to come on.

Flash began to step forward into the room, but was stopped in mid-stride by a sight that made his blood run cold. A moment later a warning siren began shrieking, and bright red lights in the corridor began flashing. Zarkov rushed through the door and grabbed Flash's arm to try to pull him back, but suddenly he too stopped.

The two of them stood blocking the wide door, looking into the large room, both of them stunned into inaction, into speechlessness.

"What is it?" Dale shouted. "What's happening?"

Flash half turned back to her, his stomach heaving. "Stay out of here, Dale," he said, barely able to form the words, any words.

"Flash, what in God's name is happening?" Dale shouted, now frightened.

Zarkov had gone all the way into the room, and Dale managed to look past Flash. An instant later she moaned something, and then started to slump to the floor, her eyes rolling up in their sockets, her eyelids fluttering.

Flash grabbed her inert form, and eased her gently back out into the corridor and around the corner from the open door, then laid her on the deck.

"Guardian," Flash said, "give me a life form monitor on Dale."

"Respiration coming to normal, heart rate rapid but strong, temperature down one-tenth point."

The siren was suddenly silenced, and a moment later Zarkov was hovering over Flash's shoulder. "What happened?" he asked, his voice shaking.

Flash looked up. "She fainted. She'll be all right." He stood up and looked deeply into his old friend's eyes, which were misted over. "We'd better go back in and check it out."

Zarkov nodded, but said nothing.

"What is happening in there?" the voice of the Trans Fed spokesman blared in their helmets.

"Miss Arden fainted," Flash said, and his mind was racing. As long as they were wearing their suits, they were tied to the Guardian aboard the *Intrepid,* and therefore their every move could be monitored by the Trans Federation vessel.

"Why?" the Trans Fed spokesman snapped.

Flash made a motion as if he was taking off his helmet, and, understanding dawning on Zarkov's eyes, the scientist nodded, indicating the atmosphere was safe to breathe.

As Flash cracked his helmet seal, a faint odor of decay and moisture assailed his nostrils. He waited a moment longer, then lifted the helmet off his head, his suit's communicator and life support functions clicking off.

Zarkov had a grim smile on his face as he unsealed his own helmet and took it off. "Trans Federation started screaming the instant you broke contact. They were saying something about sending their team over here immediately."

"Can they get in?" Flash asked. The air tasted strangely metallic, as if it had been canned for a very long time, which in effect it had. But it also smelled moist, and the odor of decay was stronger now.

"I don't think so," Zarkov said. "Unless they broach the hull, which I don't believe they'll do. Not with the Federation military standing by out there. They wouldn't go that far."

"The military hasn't offered any help yet," Flash said bitterly.

"We haven't really needed any help. But if Trans Federation tries punching a hole in the hull, they'll come after them."

Dale had started to come awake, and Flash helped her to her feet, unsealed her helmet and pulled it off. For several moments she seemed disoriented, but then her eyes fluttered and she grasped Flash's arm. "They're dead."

Flash nodded. "We're going back in there. You can come with us, or you can stay out here."

"I'll stay here," she said, and she leaned back against the wall.

"Are you going to be all right?" Flash asked.

"I'll be fine. I'm just not going back in there."

"Put your helmet back on, then. Trans Fed is sending someone over to try to get in. I want you to monitor their progress, but don't tell them a thing. If anything happens that we should know about, take off your helmet and yell. We'll hear you."

She nodded uncertainly and put her helmet back on as Flash and Zarkov went back to the doorway and stepped into the deep sleep station.

It was a large room that gleamed of chrome and glass. Spotlessly white plastic glowed from the bright lights still flashing in the corridor. And now the smell of decay was much stronger.

They stood about five meters into the room between two rows of sleep stations, which were large, glass-fronted cases that when in operation would be filled with a cryogenic liquid to preserve the sleeping forms.

"This room was sterile until we broke the seal and entered it," Zarkov said, his voice cracked with emotion. "Decay wasn't possible until now. It will go fairly fast."

"They were murdered," Flash said, unable to think of anything else to say.

The sight they were surrounded with and its implications were staggering to both men.

The glass doors on all the sleep stations were open, the cryo fluid drained out, and each sleeping human, lying nude, a peaceful expression on its face, had its throat slit completely open. There was very little blood, but what had seeped from the carotid artery and jugular vein had run down the chest of each male, and between the breasts of the females. They all looked young. In the prime of health. And except for the gaping wounds, apparently sleeping, ready to be awakened at a touch.

"My God . . ." Zarkov said, the rest of the sentence choking off in his throat. He was looking toward the end of the next bay, visible through the glass cases racked back to back, six high.

Flash let his eyes follow the scientist's gaze, and at first he saw nothing. But then it suddenly struck him, and his heart thumped. One of the sleep stations was empty!

He and Zarkov hurried around the end of the bay they were standing in to the next row over, where they examined the empty sleep station. There was no blood anywhere in or around the unit, and as Zarkov continued to examine the mechanism, Flash quickly searched the entire sleep station, counting the individual units, each with its own mutilated body, the smell already becoming almost overpowering.

When he was finished he came back to where Zarkov was still examining the empty case.

"I've counted 157 bodies. Seventy-nine of them men, but only 78 women."

Zarkov straightened up, and peered up into Flash's eyes. "Her name was Sandra Debonshire," he said softly. "Two hundred years ago, she was only twenty-two." He pointed at a small metal plaque they had overlooked before attached below a control panel on the sleep station. It showed the young woman's name and birthdate as 2154. Zarkov shook his head sadly, and looked again at the empty unit. "They had started construction of this vessel six years before she was born. As a child, perhaps, she dreamed of growing up in time to be selected for this mission, all the while in orbit overhead, this vessel was under construction."

"Where is she now?" Flash asked softly.

"I don't know," Zarkov said, and he hung his head and began to weep silently. Flash put his arm around his old friend's tiny, frail shoulders and led him toward the door as Dale came rushing to the opening, screaming something about Trans Federation broaching the hull.

# CHAPTER 5

Sirens were shrieking everywhere aboard the huge ship as Flash and Dr. Zarkov rushed out of the deep sleep station, hitting the button to close the massive white door behind them.

Dale was highly agitated, and it took them several moments to calm her down sufficiently to make any sense out of what she was shouting over the noise of the sirens.

"Slowly now," Flash said, taking the young woman by the shoulders. His own heart was still pounding from what they had seen inside the deep sleep station. "What about Trans Fed?"

"They're at the airlock we entered," she shouted, gulping her words. "They said they were going to burn through the lock if we don't open it."

Flash glanced at Zarkov, who still looked white. "They've already started," he snapped, his brain racing toward a dozen different problems. "If they get all the way through, the ship's corridors will probably seal tighter than a drum."

Zarkov was nodding, his mind obviously running just as fast as Flash's. "On the way up I saw emergency seals at every level. If they actually succeed in burning through the airlock down there, the loss in atmospheric pressure would probably trigger the seals at least along the central shaft."

"All right," Flash said, trying to think out his alternatives. "Do you think you can find the control room and then figure out the sealing system and its overrides?"

"Without the data chips in Guardian's memory it will be difficult, but I can try," Zarkov said.

"I don't want to be sealed in here. We'd have to burn through too many systems to get out," Flash said. He grabbed their helmets from where they had laid them on the deck, and when they had them on, he forced a calmness into his voice.

"Guardian," he said. But there was no answer, only a steady, low-pitched whine.

"They've got her blocked off," Zarkov's voice came over Flash's suit radio. He did not seem surprised.

"Try for the control room, doctor," Flash said. "I'll go down to the hangar deck to see if I can hold them off."

"I'm coming with you," Dale said.

"You're going with your uncle," Flash snapped. "There's going to be trouble."

She had flipped open one of the deep pockets on her pressure suit, and she withdrew a laser pistol. "I figured there'd be trouble," she said. "I'm coming with you."

"There's no time to argue, Dale," Flash shouted.

"That's right," she said. "So let's go."

Flash hesitated a moment longer, but then shook his head, exasperated, and they all rushed down the corridor to the central axis shaft, Dale and Flash heading downward, and Dr. Zarkov working his way toward the upper levels.

It took several minutes to make it all the way down the shaft. A few meters away from the hangar deck opening, Flash pushed past Dale and stopped, his laser pistol in hand.

He motioned for her to wait behind him, and he eased down to the opening and peered around the corner into the hangar deck.

The sirens were shrieking loudly here, but there was no sign that anything had changed. The airlock door across the bay from them was still intact, and Flash supposed that Trans Fed's people were still working on the outer door, unless they had been bluffing.

Above, 157 men and women lay dead, their throats brutally slashed; the weight of their bodies, and Zarkov's emotional reaction, were pressing down on Flash.

Forcing those thoughts out of his mind for the moment, he pushed his way through the opening. Dale joined him as he was clicking his sole plates to the deck. He turned, and, with his helmet light on, studied the main shaft seal, desperately searching for the means to close it. If he could secure this hatch, the loss in air pressure if the airlock were broached would be confined to this deck.

For an instant he wondered how Dr. Zarkov was faring at this moment. No matter what happened down here, he wanted no harm to come to his old friend.

As in the upper corridor, the walls here were covered with wires, lights, and literally hundreds of control panels. Finally, however, Flash found a panel marked HANGAR DECK EMERGENCY SEAL. Behind a narrow glass door was a button. He smashed the glass with the butt of his pistol and hit the switch. Instantly the axis shaft hatch closed, a heavy metal door dropping into place from the bulkhead above.

Hurrying across to the still secure airlock door, Flash motioned for Dale to take up a position behind one of the shuttle craft. When she was in place, he hit the airlock button, and as the hatch began cycling open he stepped back about five meters, crouched down on one knee, and trained his laser pistol on the opening.

The door swung all the way open, and across the tiny airlock he could see the outer door glowing a cherry red. Trans Fed's people were actually burning through the lock.

"Trans Federation Executive," Flash said into his suit radio. "Do you read me?"

"Be careful, Flash," Dale's voice came over his suit radio, and he glanced her way. She looked determined.

A spot of white appeared at the center of the outer airlock door, and the metal began to crumble.

"Trans Federation Executive, this is Colonel Gordon. I'm warning you to stand off."

The outer airlock door suddenly collapsed and then blew outward as the hangar deck explosively decompressed, the screaming wind nearly knocking Flash over.

"Trans Fed," Flash shouted into his suit radio. "Stand off or we will use force."

A pressure suited figure appeared in the airlock opening and, spotting Flash, raised a laser rifle and began firing from the hip as he leapt through the airlock.

Flash returned the fire, then dove to the right toward the shuttle craft as a second man pushed his way into the airlock, the first man going down on the deck, his helmet disintegrated.

A section of the shuttle craft above Flash exploded, sending bits of molten metal sputtering on the deck, and the second man fell backward against the airlock door, writhing in agony. There was a gaping hole burned through his shoulder, and the life supports on his suit were winking off.

Flash looked up as Dale dove around the edge of the shuttle craft he was under and took up a new position behind one of the craft's launching ramps.

"Colonel Gordon," a voice called over his suit radio. "Do you read?"

Flash lay flat on the deck, his pistol aimed at the open airlock, the bodies of the two men sprawled in a heap. He quickly switched channels on his suit radio. "Federation Military Command. Federation Military Command. Do you read?"

"Communications with the military have been blocked off," Flash's suit radio blared on the new channel. "We are asking you to abandon the *Goodhope*. We will stand off and allow you to leave peacefully."

"Release my Guardian channel to me," Flash said as he tried to think this out. At this point there was no way Trans Fed would let them go alive. And yet their deaths would have to seem like an accident, or at least as if the Trans Fed people had

been doing nothing more than defending themselves. Yet none of this made any sense. Trans Federation had a legitimate claim on the *Goodhope*. All
they would have had to do was permit Dr. Zarkov
to conduct his investigation and allow the bodies of
the crew and passengers to be taken Earthside for
a decent burial, and the ship would have been
theirs. Why they were taking this kind of risk with
the Federation Military standing nearby was a
mystery.

"I'm afraid we can't do that, Colonel Gordon.
But we will allow you to board your vessel and
leave peacefully."

"Negative," Flash said into his suit radio. "It
has gone too far for that now. We're going to remain here. Sooner or later the military will wonder
what's happening, and will come to investigate."

"You leave us no other choice, then, Colonel
Gordon. We mean to take control of the
*Goodhope*, and will do so once we have the military convinced that you and your party have died
aboard your own vessel when it explodes."

Flash leapt up and propelled himself toward the
open airlock, catching the edge of the hatch with
his left hand while holding his laser pistol at the
ready in his right. He eased his way over the bodies
of the two dead Trans Federation men, pushed into
the airlock, and cautiously edged toward the outer
airlock hatch, which had been completely burned
away.

He was in time to see a Trans Federation shuttle
craft moving away, and a moment later the *Intrepid*
began dropping from the *Goodhope*'s landing
blister.

"Federation Military Command! Federation Military Command! Do you hear?" Flash shouted into his suit radio. But there was no response, and he watched helplessly as the *Intrepid* began to turn slowly. Her reaction engines came on once she was around, and in a brilliant glare she dropped out of sight toward a lower orbit.

"Flash," Dr. Zarkov's voice blared in his suit radio.

He turned and pushed his way back through the airlock onto the hangar deck. "Where are you, doctor?" he said, stepping over the two bodies. Dale had come out from behind the shuttle craft, and stood holding her laser pistol.

"I'm in the control room. It's about thirty decks above the sleep station level through a hatch marked HELM. You and Dale had better get up here."

"The main shaft is sealed. The hangar deck is in a hard vacuum."

"Wait a minute," Zarkov said, and Flash could hear a note of deep concern in his voice. Then he was back. "I'm showing an open airlock. Can you seal it?"

"Yes," Flash said.

"Do it right now," Zarkov snapped. "I can repressurize the hangar deck from here. But hurry— there isn't much time!"

"What is it, Uncle Hans?" Dale said. She was looking around her, almost as if she expected someone or something to leap out of the shadows at her. "What's happening?"

"There's no time for that now, Dale. Just do as I say. And please, hurry."

Without hesitation Flash shoved both bodies out the airlock, then hit the hatch control. The large door ponderously swung closed on its massive hinges, its seals matching, and a moment later the airlock control board winked green.

"The airlock is sealed," Flash said.

"Pressurization cycle has begun. Get the axis shaft hatch open and get up here, now!" Zarkov shouted.

Flash and Dale rushed to the rear of the hangar deck and, rapidly scanning the various control panels near the hatch, Flash found the proper control for opening it. A light above the button, however, showed red, moisture condensing on the metal work from air streaming through the vents.

Finally the hatch light winked green as the pressure came up to normal on the hangar deck, and Flash hit the button, the door sliding smoothly up into the overhead.

"Hurry," Zarkov's voice blared in Flash's suit radio, as he and Dale leapt into the shaft.

Flash pushed her straight up, and, grabbing a handhold, frantically searched for a hatch control there inside the shaft, finding it above the door frame. He hit the close button, and the hatch once again sealed itself.

"We're in the shaft, and it's sealed," Flash shouted as he sprung up, catching Dale and pulling her along with him up the tube.

Lights came on all along the shaft, and a bell began stridently clanging far above them. Below, just above the hangar deck, an iris diaphragm closed, sealing the lower level off from the landing blister area.

A moment later another iris diaphragm closed, this one just above the first deck opening; as fast as Flash and Dale rose up the axis shaft, the diaphragms were being sealed deck by deck behind them.

"What's happening up there?!" Flash shouted.

"The *Intrepid* just exploded, Flash, and the military is heading down to it. But Trans Federation has moved their ship into position off the hangar blister below you."

"Is there any way of getting off the ship from where you are?"

"Not now," Zarkov said, and it sounded as if he was under some kind of extreme strain. "Hurry, Flash!" he shouted. "It looks as if this ship is sequencing for takeoff and I can't do anything about it!"

Without hesitation, they passed the main corridor off which the sleep station was located, that deck sealing off behind them like the others.

An explosion from somewhere below vibrated off the shaft's bulkheads, and a moment later the gigantic ship seemed to come alive with a low-pitched hum that could only be felt, not heard. The lights dimmed once, then twice, and the hum climbed in pitch.

Flash renewed his efforts, hauling himself up the handholds as fast as he possibly could, the sweat streaming down his forehead as his suit's cooling unit fell behind the demand. Dale was moving up the shaft just as fast as he was, and slightly above him.

"T MINUS THIRTY SECONDS AND SEQUENCING," a flat, emotionless mechanical voice echoed down the axis shaft, and the lights dimmed even further as the hum that vibrated through the ship rose higher up the scale.

Dale was beginning to slow down, worn out from the exertion. None of them had slept in the last twenty-four hours, and Flash's body was a mass of aches from the battering he had taken in the Tri-V match just a few hours ago.

Another explosion reverberated up the shaft from somewhere below, and then Dr. Zarkov's suited figure appeared from a hatch about fifty meters above them.

"Trans Federation has blown the hangar deck main door," Zarkov's voice blared in Flash's suit radio.

"T MINUS TWENTY SECONDS. FINAL SEQUENCING COMMENCING," the toneless voice boomed down the shaft over the clanging bell.

With a final heave Flash shoved Dale above him, and as she floated up to the helm deck hatch, Zarkov grabbed her arm and pulled her unceremoniously into the corridor; Flash joined them a moment later.

The narrow passageway, which led sharply uphill away from the axis shaft, was jammed with old-fashioned electronic equipment; banks of flashing lights and hundreds of gauges and dials, were all indicating that the ship had, for some reason, suddenly come alive after lying dormant for perhaps a hundred years or more.

"T MINUS TEN SECONDS ..." the voice blared, much closer, with no echo here in these confined quarters. "... NINE ... EIGHT ..."

Dr. Zarkov was moving as fast as his old legs would propel him up the corridor, pushing Dale ahead of him. A few meters away from the axis shaft, which had sealed itself, he shoved Dale through a narrow oval opening between banks of equipment, and ducked inside himself.

"... SEVEN ... SIX ... FIVE ..."

Flash shoved his way through the oval hatch into a large room that was crammed with a bewildering array of ancient equipment, and at least a dozen acceleration couches. Dale and Dr. Zarkov both were strapping themselves into couches near the forward end of the room, below a dozen visiscreens, which showed various views outside the ship.

"... FOUR ... THREE ... TWO ..." the voice blared as Flash dropped into an acceleration couch next to Dr. Zarkov and fumbled with the old-fashioned restraining devices.

"... ONE ... ZERO ..." And the ship began to move, ponderously at first, but then faster and faster, the acceleration shoving the three of them deeply into their heavily cushioned, gimballed chairs.

The equipment came alive, and Flash, still wearing his pressure suit and helmet, thought he heard Trans Fed shouting something, but it seemed as if it was coming from very far away, over a lot of heavy static.

And suddenly a high-pitched whine rose up in volume, blotting out all other sounds and nearly all reason, as a harsh wave of nausea swept through Flash's body. Through a dim haze in his vision he watched the forward visiscreen on the bulkhead above him as the stars seemed to grow and blossom into one huge multi-colored kaleidoscope of fantastic brilliance.

Just before he lost consciousness he realized with shock that they were going into hyper drive aboard a ship that had been constructed a hundred and fifty years before hyper drive propulsion had been invented.

# CHAPTER 6

"What is it?" Dale Arden asked.

She, Flash, and Dr. Zarkov stood on a narrow catwalk overlooking the *Goodhope*'s drive room. The distant wall was at least 500 meters away, and below them it was at least 75 meters to the main deck. Huge cables, ductwork, and other pieces of massive equipment seemed to run helter skelter with no apparent design or purpose.

"I don't know yet," Zarkov said.

Directly in the center of the mammoth cavern of a room, where one of the four main fusion generators should have been located, was an irregularly shaped mass of what appeared to be common granite. It seemed to be nothing more than a huge boulder set amidst the other equipment, surrounded by a dull blue glow.

The three of them stared down at the odd sight below them, and from time to time Dr. Zarkov studied a series of blueprints he had found three days ago.

It had been exactly one week since they had unexpectedly left Earth orbit, and during that time they had managed to explore much of the ship and figure out many of the ship's systems. But from their explorations they had gained no clues as to why the ship had suddenly come to life, where they were going, where Sandra Debonshire, the missing woman from the cryo sleep station, had disappeared to, or who had killed the remaining 157 men and women and why.

One thing was definite, however, and that was that the *Goodhope* was falling apart. In their explorations they had come across old-fashioned electric motors that had burned up, bearings that had seized for lack of maintenance, electronic equipment rendered useless because of malfunctioned components that could take years to figure out how to repair; and now this.

Zarkov looked up from the blueprints he was studying and shook his head. "Whatever it is, it wasn't included in the original design."

"It's the hyper drive unit," Flash said, gazing down at the strange object.

"Obviously," Zarkov said, without sarcasm. "But who installed it, and when?"

"Or why?" Dale added, and the comment suddenly made Flash uncomfortable.

He began to wonder whether or not this had been some kind of a Trans Fed setup from the beginning, but he dismissed the idea quickly. That thing below them, whatever it was, definitely was beyond even Trans Fed. If indeed it was the hyper drive unit, it was a device that no one in the Federation, including Trans Fed, could have come up with.

Besides the fact that it did not look like anything he had ever seen of Federation manufacture, the device had kept them in continuous hyper drive for a solid week now, whereas normal hyper drive jumps lasted no more than a second or two. Usually time in transit was burned up by sub-light drive from catalogued hyper point to catalogued hyper point.

Flash was bothered by something else as well. The bodies in the deep sleep station. He had gone back to that deck two days ago with his pressure suit on and his helmet sealed, drawn for some irresistible reason to the scene of what they all were calling the massacre.

And it had been grim. Much worse than he had expected it to be. Because of the bacteria their presence had introduced to the sterile room, the decay had gone quite quickly, and the sight when he had entered the room had been seared into his mind's eye. Last night and the night before he had not slept well. Every time he closed his eyes he saw the bodies of the men and women, their flesh rotted away, the gaping wounds in their necks; and there was a young woman wielding a knife that was dripping with blood; she was screaming and laughing insanely.

"This is how I see it," Zarkov was saying, and Flash turned his attention to the scientist. "Although I'd like to get down there for a closer look, it's not worth the effort."

Flash said nothing, the remnants of his nightmare still at the back of his mind.

"The circuitry for the hatches on all levels below this point is shorted out, and it would take more power than our weapons have left to burn through them. The main axis shaft comes close at this level, but we'd still have to burn through a half dozen bulkheads to make it down there."

"How about climbing down on a line?" Dale asked, and Flash had to wonder why he had not thought of that.

But Zarkov was shaking his head. "I don't think I'd care to drop in on top of that thing."

Dale looked down over the railing and nodded her agreement.

"Besides," Zarkov said, "I don't have the equipment to figure out what the thing is anyway. And just looking at it isn't going to tell us much."

Flash tried to shake his premonitions of disaster from his mind, but was without success. "So, we're stuck in hyper space until that thing decides to bring us out, wherever that might be," he said.

"That's about it, Flash," Zarkov said, looking up at him. "At least we're away from Trans Fed for the time being."

Flash laughed in spite of himself. "I'm getting to the point where I'd almost welcome a couple of Trans Fed's people sneaking up behind me to take a shot!"

No one said anything for several long moments. In the silence they were all drawn to look down again at the device in the center of the drive room.

"No one in the Federation built that," Dale said finally, in a hushed voice.

Zarkov turned to his niece. "No, they didn't," he said, and he looked at his watch. It was shortly after ten in the evening in western North America— the time standard they all had slept and wakened on. "There's nothing more for us to do here, so I think I'll turn in. Tomorrow we can try again with the Central Data Bank. Now that we know this thing is here . . . whatever it is . . . we can ask the shipboard computer if it knows anything about the mechanism."

"You don't expect anything from that, do you, doctor?" Flash asked.

Zarkov shook his head tiredly. "No," he said, and he turned toward the hatch. "Are you two coming?"

"In a minute," Flash said, looking at Dale.

Zarkov turned back, then glanced down at the device below them on the drive room floor. "Don't try to go down there, Flash. We have no way of telling what might happen."

"What do you mean?" Flash said, trying to cover his feelings of guilt. It had been exactly his intention. He had planned doing what Dale had suggested—climb down to the unit on a line, if for no other reason than merely to look around. Perhaps if the unit itself would yield no clues its method of installation might.

Zarkov's eyes seemed to glaze over and he took several long seconds to answer. "That device came as no real surprise to me. The only surprise was its location. I guessed it would have been located in or around the ship's central control bank, not here." He looked over the rail.

"What are you talking about, doc?" Flash asked, moving a step closer to the old man.

Zarkov looked up. "When Trans Federation's people were coming after us, and I went up to the control room, I stumbled across the fusion generator monitoring board. The generators were all but dead."

"Impossible," Flash said, not understanding.

"There was barely enough power left for life supports and a few sensory devices. Nothing else."

"What are you saying?" Flash asked, a sudden cold feeling spreading inside of him.

"There was no power for the engines, or the control systems, and yet we took off."

"It's a hyper drive unit," Flash said, nodding toward the device below them.

"It's more than that. I touched nothing while I was on the bridge except the fusion generator monitoring board, and then the life support console. *Nothing* other than that."

"You must have hit some switch. Something that automatically started the takeoff sequence."

Zarkov was shaking his head. "No, Flash. I touched nothing." Again he looked down at the device glowing a soft blue. "That thing sensed Trans Federation's attack and got us out of there. Or should I say, got itself out of there."

"It's a Guardian computer," Dale said in a hushed tone.

"That and more," Zarkov said. "This device, besides providing hyper drive capabilities, is now providing all the power for this ship. All the power, and that includes life supports. As of early this morning the fusion generators were completely cold. I would guess they simply ran out of material for conversion. Probably part of the crew's responsibilities was to replenish the hydrogen supply."

"We're completely at that thing's mercy," Dale said.

"Or the mercy of whoever built it," Zarkov corrected, looking sternly at his niece. Then he turned to Flash again. "Which is why I don't think it would be wise to go down there and tamper with it. At the worst it would shut itself off, and we'd be totally without power and life supports. We'd all die. At the least it would kill you to keep you from tampering with it."

"Why didn't it take evasive action when the *Aras'Z'Eata* took the ship in tow?" Flash asked.

Zarkov shook his head. "I don't know. Perhaps it didn't consider a tow much of a threat, but somehow objected to Trans Federation burning holes in its plates."

"So we just sit around and wait for whatever happens?" Dale asked, her voice rising slightly in pitch.

Zarkov took her hands in his. "I'm afraid there's little else we can do, my dear. But I think that device's primary function is the safety of this vessel. So as long as we don't interfere with its functions, we'll be fine. Just fine."

"Are you sure, uncle?" Dale asked, looking into the old man's eyes.

He smiled wanly. "As sure as I can possibly be under these trying circumstances," he said. Then he seemed to shake himself out of his morose mood. "And now I think we should all turn in. Who knows what tomorrow might bring."

"We'll be right with you, doctor," Flash said, and Zarkov looked sharply at him.

"I won't go down there," Flash said, holding up his hands. "Promise."

Zarkov laughed, and patted Flash on the arm.

"It's like keeping the cat away from the cream," he said, but he turned and went through the hatch, leaving Flash and Dale alone on the narrow catwalk.

They said nothing to each other at first, their eyes drawn once again, irresistibly, toward the thing below them. For a moment Flash wondered about the bodies in the deep sleep station. If Dr. Zarkov was correct, and the device below them was like a sophisticated Guardian computer as well as a hyper drive unit and power station all in one, had it sensed the killings? Or had the device been installed after the crew and passengers had been murdered?

Dale seemed almost to be reading his thoughts. "Do you think whoever installed that thing had anything to do with the murders of the crew and passengers?"

Flash jumped out of his thoughts and looked at her. "I don't know," he said, "but I'd guess not. Someone or something sophisticated enough to design and build something like that would not be so crude as to murder the crew and passengers by slitting their throats. The machine could have merely directed the computer to shut off the life supports on the cryo units."

Dale looked up into Flash's eyes. "You and Uncle Hans found something in the deep sleep station. Something besides the 158 bodies."

For a moment what she was asking him was not registering. He was seeing her, it almost seemed, for the first time. And he had the urge to reach out, take her in his arms, and hold her close to comfort himself as well as her.

"What?" he said, pulling himself out of his thoughts.

Dale stamped her foot. "I asked you a question," she snapped. "You and Uncle Hans found something other than 158 bodies in the deep sleep station. What was it?"

"One hundred and fifty-seven bodies," Flash corrected.

"What?"

"There was one body missing. A woman by the name of Sandra Debonshire."

"My God, that's horrible," Dale said. "She was the murderer?"

Flash shrugged. "We don't know. All we know is that she's missing, and we've found no trace of her so far aboard this ship."

Dale reflexively looked over her shoulder and shivered. "What do you suppose happened to her?"

For a brief instant a wave of deep affection for Dale washed through Flash, but then it was replaced by irritation that she had talked her way into coming along. She was one more thing he had to worry about. "I don't know," he said crossly, and he started to turn away, but Dale reached out and turned him back with her hand on his arm.

"Flash, most of the time I put up a good front, but I'm frightened now," she said, looking into his eyes.

"I told you to stay behind," Flash snapped.

"I wanted to be with you," she said softly, and she turned her eyes away.

Touched, Flash was about to reach for her, when suddenly a siren began whooping and a powerful whine rose up from the device below them.

"What's happening?" Dale screamed over the din.

The unit on the drive room floor had suddenly turned a violently deep shade of blue—so intense that it hurt the eyes.

"I don't know for sure," Flash shouted over the noise, grabbing Dale's arm and hauling her bodily through the hatch. "I think we're getting ready to come out of hyper drive."

They ran up the corridor, which curved sharply toward the hull about a hundred meters away, finally coming to a monorail shuttle still in its cradle.

The central axis shaft, they had discovered during their first day of exploration aboard, was designed to be used as nothing more than an emergency escape route from anywhere in the ship if power failed and the ship had to be abandoned.

Normal transportation through the vast bulk of the ship, which was larger than many small towns, was via a network of miniature monorails with stations scattered at various spots on every deck. It was a crude but effective system.

Flash unceremoniously shoved Dale in the rear seat and leapt onto the front seat, punched the button for the helm deck, and the transport took off along the rail that circled the inner hull.

"FLASH . . . DALE . . . WHERE ARE YOU?" the ship's PA system blared over the whooping siren.

Flash reached out and punched the communicator button on the simple control console in front of him. "We're on our way to the helm!" he shouted.

"We're sequencing out of hyper drive," Dr.

Zarkov's voice came over the communicator.
"Hurry!"

Flash reached out to flip off the intercom when
the first wave of dizziness and nausea clutched at
his insides. Behind him he was dimly aware that
Dale was screaming, the noise of the sirens nearly
drowning out her cries. He tried to turn in his seat,
but another wave of nausea gripped him, and he
was flung violently forward, slamming his head
against the console.

He fought for consciousness, his entire body
screaming in protest—then, as suddenly as the
sickness had come, it was gone, leaving him dazed
and somewhat disoriented.

The monorail car was slowing to a halt as Flash
managed to sit upright, a thin trickle of blood running down from a small cut on his forehead. His
head was throbbing, but the dizziness and nausea
were gone. Evidently they had come out of hyper
space, and as the car stopped it occurred to him
that the ship was silent. The siren had stopped . . .
and, he suddenly realized, so had Dale's screams.

He whirled around in his seat in time to see Dale
slump over the side onto the deck. A moment later
he was out of his seat and beside her, gently pulling
her away from the transport.

Her eyelids were fluttering, and for a moment
she tried to say something, but then she suddenly
sat up wretching, and she vomited, Flash holding
her frail shoulders.

"Flash!" Zarkov shouted from behind them.

Flash turned around as Zarkov rushed up the
corridor from the helm bay, out of breath and
white-faced.

Dale had recovered sufficiently for Flash to help her to her feet by the time Zarkov made it up to them.

"We've got to abandon ship!" Zarkov shouted breathlessly.

"Take it easy, Doc," Flash said. "What's happened?"

"We came out of hyper space less than twenty thousand kilometers from a planet. We're heading in right now. But something is wrong."

Flash gripped Zarkov's arm. "What's wrong? Where are we?"

"The astrogation computer is working it out right now. But the ship's controls have burned up. She doesn't answer to yaw or pitch. We're heading for a crash landing."

Dale was still a little unsteady on her feet, but Flash left her in the corridor and followed Zarkov in a dead run back to the helm. The forward visi-screens were up and showed a yellowish-green planet directly ahead. They were close enough already that the planet completely filled the screens set at their lowest power magnification. Red lights were winking all across several consoles.

"The ship is breaking up," Zarkov shouted. "Something has gone wrong. Instead of going into orbit, we're going straight in. And this ship wasn't designed for that kind of strain."

Several alarms were beginning to sound over the growing noise at the hull of the ship straining against the planet's atmosphere. And then a chime sounded across the bridge from where they stood. Zarkov turned and rushed over to a low console that was covered with clear plastic enclosing a deep well. Inside the well was a black sphere dotted with complicated patterns of tiny lights. Numbers streamed across a small data screen on the side of the unit, and as Flash joined Zarkov, the unit chimed a second time. Zarkov punched several buttons next to the data screen, and a star pattern suddenly appeared on the black sphere.

A moment later Zarkov looked up. "Gama Andromedae," he said in a hushed voice. "It's an orange KO type star 165 light-years from Earth."

"In one week?" Flash asked flabbergasted. Even with catalogued hyper points, it took the fastest military vessel six or seven months to make the rim of the Federation, which was barely 100 light-years from Earth. They had gone half again that far in a fraction of the time.

"We'll never make orbit," Zarkov snapped.

"How about the hangar blister?" Flash asked. "Is there any way from here of pressurizing it so we can get to the shuttle craft?"

Zarkov was shaking his head, his fingers playing over the keyboard on another console in front of one of the acceleration couches. "The main hangar door was burned away. No way of pressurizing that deck now." He looked up. "We don't even know if the shuttle craft are still intact. When Trans Federation blew their way on board there is a good chance they destroyed our only chance of escape."

Flash's mind was racing, and as he tried to think, another siren began whooping; nearly every console on the helm was already ablaze with red warning indicators.

"It's our only chance of getting out of here,"

Flash shouted over the sirens. "Depressurize the main axis shaft and open all the ship's hatches."

Dale had come onto the helm and Flash rushed back to her, shouting, "Get into your pressure suit."

For a moment she didn't seem to understand what he was saying, so he grabbed up one of the suits they had laid over an acceleration couch near the hatch and helped her pull it on. Then he got into his own suit, and grabbed Zarkov's as the old man hurried back to them.

"The main shaft is depressurized, but the hatches won't hold long. The circuitry is being overridden by the emergency failsafes."

"Then we don't have much time," Flash said as he helped Zarkov into his bulky one-piece pressure suit. They yanked on their helmets, and when they had them sealed Flash led them back out into the corridor and down to the monorail transport.

Dale and Zarkov crowded onto the back seat and Flash took the front, punching the controls for the lowest deck on the ship, which was just one deck up from the hangar blister, and the transport took off.

Other sirens throughout the ship were wailing now, and the lights began to grow dimmer as the power takeoff units strained against impossible odds to maintain ship integrity.

It took them less than four minutes to make it to the bottom deck, which consisted mostly of electrical and plumbing runs. As the transport slowed to a halt, the ship's lights flickered and then died completely, plunging them into total darkness.

Flash flipped on his suit lights, and a moment

later Dale and Zarkov's suit lights came on as well.
They piled off the transport and raced down the
corridor toward the center of the ship, as a series of
explosions reverberated off the bulkheads from
somewhere far above them. The ship was in its
death throes.

They came finally to an airtight hatch that led to
the main axis shaft, and Flash positioned Dale and
Zarkov about twenty meters away. He hurried
back to the hatch, pulling his laser pistol from its
holster and setting it on its highest power. The
weapon's charge had been severely depleted by the
two fire fights he had been in and by the several
hatches he had burned through during their exploration of the ship, but in less than sixty seconds
he managed to burn through the hinges and main
locking mechanism. He braced himself as the airtight door began to sag into its frame, then suddenly it blew open with a bang, the decompression
slamming Flash forward and into the axis shaft.

At the last moment he grabbed a handhold in the
shaft, and, in a steady gale of ship's air rushing past
him, worked his way back up the shaft. When he
had emerged he helped Dale and Zarkov through
the opening.

They moved slowly, hand over hand, down the
shaft to the hangar deck hatch, which had been
burned away. Trans Federation's people had
evidently gotten this far when the ship had gone
into hyper drive, and for just a brief instant Flash
felt sorry for the poor devils who had been caught
down here when the ship had suddenly taken off.

Flash was the first through the hangar blister
hatch, and the sight that greeted him took his

breath away. In the dim light he could just make out a twisted pile of metal, wire, and plastic where the shuttle craft had been. Beyond them, the main hangar door was gone, and through the opening he could see the planet rushing up toward them, close enough now so that he could make out weather patterns, and below the clouds, continents and at least one major sea.

# CHAPTER 7

The massive bulk of the *Goodhope* had begun to tumble in the turbulent upper atmosphere by the time Flash had managed to climb over the wreckage of the first two shuttle craft in line. The heat from skin friction was building up rapidly and his suit's coolant pump was whining angrily. He shone his light past the blasted open cockpit of the third shuttle craft and for a moment his heart hammered wildly in his chest. But then he scrambled closer to the fourth craft. It was not damaged as far as he could tell. If they could get it launched they would have a chance to survive at least until they made planetfall.

"The last craft is intact," he shouted over his suit radio.

Dale had climbed over the wreckage right behind him, and she too shone her light on the last shuttle craft in line.

"Is it blocked by the wreckage?" Zarkov's voice

came over their suit radios.

"Can't tell from here," Flash said. "I'll have to climb down to it."

"Hurry, Flash, there isn't much time," Zarkov said, his voice urgent.

Flash climbed over the third shuttle craft, skirting the gaping hole that led into the charred remnants of the cockpit, and on the other side jumped down to the deck beside the fourth craft.

The explosions had pushed the second and third shuttle boats off their launchers, and now the lower struts of the third one was blocking the fourth launch track.

"The launch track is blocked," Flash radioed to Zarkov. "But I think I can burn it clear."

"I'm coming over," Zarkov radioed.

The tumbling of the huge spacecraft, becoming more and more violent, was shifting the apparent gravitational center of the ship erratically in all directions, making it nearly impossible to maintain any kind of balance.

Nevertheless Zarkov managed to work his way over the wreckage of the three destroyed shuttle craft where Flash and Dale helped him down to the deck. He quickly surveyed the track, then went down on his hands and knees to check clearance over the rest of the launch equipment.

"Go ahead and burn it away," he said finally, straightening up. "But be careful not to burn a hole in the hull."

Flash pulled out his laser gun as Zarkov went aft along the hull of the shuttle craft, did something with a control panel set flush in the outer skin, and then pulled a wide hatch open.

"I've got the main hatch open, Flash," Zarkov radioed. "I'll go aboard and get ready for launch. Hurry."

Flash began burning away the twisted shuttle craft landing struts that were blocking the track, but his laser was nearly out of charge, and the work was going slowly. Too slowly.

Dale pulled out her laser, and fired it in a steady charge around the back side of the strut, the metal glowing a deep cherry red. Finally the strut began to weaken and bend away from the track.

Flash reached out and kicked the hot metal, pushing it away from the track, and he and Dale rushed back to the open hatch and climbed aboard. The track was clear, but the strut and other wreckage was very close to the launch track, and still could cause them trouble.

They pulled the hatch cover shut, and dogged the latches, and a moment later the shuttle craft's power and lights came on.

Flash and Dale worked their way forward and just managed to strap themselves into the seats on the bridge next to Zarkov when the *Goodhope* lurched to the port, and then began to tumble even more wildly, shoving their shuttle craft half off its launch track.

"We're off the track," Zarkov shouted, flipping the craft's launch sequence switches back off. "We'll never make it."

"Yes, we will," Flash shouted, overriding Zarkov's controls. The shuttle craft panel was simple, of necessity. People in stress did not have time to think about sequencing. As a result emergency shuttles were always constructed simply, so that even a deeply confused person, or someone like Flash who had never seen these kinds of controls, could operate one with ease.

Flash hit the sequencing buttons for takeoff, and hit the power booster. A moment later the craft's engine screamed wildly up the scale, the shuttle lurching and jumping.

"No!" Dale screamed.

"We'll explode!" Zarkov shouted.

But Flash raised the power booster all the way to its stops, and an instant later the *Goodhope* began breaking apart, flipping over on its forward face, spilling the shuttle craft and most of the wreckage out of the hangar opening, and they were out, accelerating away from the *Goodhope*'s bulk, still tumbling and twisting madly above them.

Flash held the acceleration full on until at long last they cleared the underside of the *Goodhope* and still he continued angling slowly planetward, skimming the edges of the thick, atmosphere.

Behind them the *Goodhope* was breaking up faster now, flames and explosions everywhere across its mind-boggling bulk, huge sections flying away, spinning and tumbling toward the sea below them.

And then the huge ship ignited in a brilliant white flare that sent the shuttle craft spinning wildly out of control.

Flash desperately hung on to the acceleration booster, holding the five-G pressure as the unusual forces on the tiny craft threatened to buckle the bulkheads and crush the hull.

Another tremendous explosion aboard what remained of the *Goodhope*'s bulk completely broke

up the remnants of the once huge vessel, sending
millions of pieces scattering toward the planet's
surface. From below it must have looked like a major meteor shower, the huge pieces of the ship
glowing, then burning up in the atmosphere. And
finally it was over. Nothing remained of the
*Goodhope* except traces of metal and, below them,
flashes of light and vapor trails in the lower atmosphere.

At 100 kilometers above the surface, Flash managed to bring the shuttle craft back to some
semblance of control, although the explosions on
the *Goodhope* so close to them had all but made
any control impossible.

Below them was a vast expanse of green, which
even from this height they could distinguish as forest or jungle, and some distance to the east was the
edge of the sea they had spotted earlier.

Flash tried to angle toward the seacoast, but the
craft was not responding quickly enough for them
to make it all the way. Twenty kilometers, he esti-
mated their probable landing site would be from
the seacoast. Twenty kilometers of unknown
jungle.

At ten kilometers above the surface the shuttle
craft's automatic sequencing board fired the roll,
pitch, and yaw retro-rockets, properly positioning
them for landing, and slowing them down.

At five kilometers, a second bank of retro-rockets fired automatically, and the craft slowed still
further.

"I've got an atmospheric out of this thing,"
Zarkov's voice came over their suit radios.

Flash turned momentarily away from the control board. Zarkov was working with an overhead console of some kind, and he glanced over at Flash.

"It's within acceptable limits for us. Rich in oxygen and carbon dioxide. Low on nitrogen. Gravity .85 Earth normal. Water vapor content is high. Around 90 percent relative humidity, with a temperature of a bit over twenty-five degrees celsius. Hot and wet."

The shuttle craft suddenly lurched to the starboard, and a short, sharp explosion rocked the back end somewhere in the vicinity of the engine compartment, and they began to fall and tumble, totally out of control.

"What happened?" Dale screamed.

"We lost our engine," Flash shouted over the growing hum and whine of the wind against their hull.

Zarkov unstrapped his seat harness and with great difficulty rolled out of his seat onto the wildly pitching deck. Flash thought the old man had fallen out of his seat and he reached over to help him, but Zarkov brushed away Flash's hands and grappled with a panel set in the deck. In a second he had it open and pulled up on a pair of red handles.

An instant later the shuttle craft lurched, slowed for a few seconds, but then began rapidly accelerating again. Zarkov reached down and pulled a second pair of red handles.

"Wind resistance devices," he said, panting. "They called them parachutes. I remembered seeing the word once."

Again the shuttle craft lurched, but this time the

chutes held, and they slowed down, swinging beneath two huge parachutes in the heavy, rich atmosphere.

Zarkov managed to crawl back up in his seat and rebuckle his harness as they came through a layer of clouds, bumping and lurching in the turbulence.

"Tighten your harnesses, we're going to come in hard," he shouted over their suit radios.

Flash turned in his seat to make sure that Dale had properly tightened her harness, and then he tightened his own.

Through the thick forward ports, they could see the jungle coming up at them, far too fast for any margin of safety, and at the last minute Flash took a final bearing on the distant seacoast, and then braced himself.

"Hang on!" he shouted, and the shuttle craft, swinging on the huge parachutes above them crashed through the first branches of the trees, several hundred meters above the ground, and then plowed its way downward, heeling over at the last instant, and slamming on its side into the ground.

Immediately the back end of the shuttle craft caught fire, and, although he was somewhat dazed, Flash managed to unbuckle his harness and climb out of his seat.

Dale was all right, but Zarkov was unconscious, blood trickling from the corner of his mouth.

Flash unstrapped the scientist and eased him out of the seat. He followed Dale back to the main hatch, the craft rapidly filling with smoke. He laid Zarkov on the sharply slanting deck and with Dale's help they managed to manually undo the hatch and force it upward and out on its bent frame.

He helped Dale up through the hatch opening, and when she was standing on the shuttle craft's outer hull, he eased Zarkov's frail form up through the hatch to her, and then climbed up himself.

A small explosion racked the back end of the shuttle as Flash helped Dale down over the side of the hull to the ground and lowered Zarkov's still inert form to her, jumping down to them a second later.

The shuttle craft had knocked down several large trees and crushed the undergrowth, creating a narrow opening in what appeared to be a nearly impenetrable jungle.

With Zarkov over his shoulder and his nearly exhausted laser pistol in his left hand, Flash headed away from the burning shuttle craft, cutting his way through the undergrowth with short bursts from his pistol.

They had managed to go less than fifty meters when a large explosion completely destroyed the remains of the shuttle craft, and Dale and Flash stood looking down the narrow alley they had cut through the underbrush at their last contact with Earth, 165 light-years away.

Dale shivered and Zarkov began to stir. Flash gently laid the old man down on the soft ground, then unsealed the scientist's helmet and took it off. Zarkov gasped with the fresh, oxygen-rich air, and his eyes fluttered and opened.

Flash took off his own helmet and laid it on the ground. "How do you feel, Doc?"

Zarkov managed a slight smile. "Now that I know we made it in one piece, I feel pretty good."

Dale had taken off her helmet as well, and she knelt down beside her uncle and helped him sit up.

"Are you sure you're all right, Uncle Hans?"

Zarkov patted his niece on the arm. "Just a little shook up, my dear. Old men like me aren't supposed to get this much exercise. I'll be all right as soon as I catch my breath, although I don't believe I'll be doing any handstands today."

They all laughed, more from relief than anything else, and Zarkov looked beyond Dale and Flash, down the path they had cut through the thick undergrowth at the furiously burning shuttle craft. Then he looked up again at Flash, the smile gone from his lips.

"Did you get a relative bearing to the seacoast?"

Flash nodded. "Almost due east from here, but it's at least twenty kilometers away."

"We were coming up fairly close on the terminator. Nightfall is probably only an hour or so away. We'd better stay here for the night, and start out at first light."

Flash and Dale helped the aging scientist to his feet.

"Why the seacoast?" Dale asked.

"If there's any civilization on this planet, the chances of finding it will be greater along a seacoast than inland. And it will be much easier to travel along an open beach than through this jungle."

"We didn't see any signs of civilization on the way down," Dale said, a slight hysterical edge to her voice. She pushed a strand of hair away from her face and looked again back at the shuttle craft. The fire was starting to subside.

"We didn't have time to do a proper search," Zarkov said soothingly.

She turned back to him. "We're stuck here, uncle. We're stuck here for the rest of our lives. This planet is sixty-five light-years from the nearest Federation outpost. And that's across uncatalogued space. They couldn't find us even if they knew what direction we had gone . . ."

"You're forgetting one thing, Dale," Zarkov gently cut her off.

Tears were starting to well up in her eyes, but she stifled a sob and held her silence, waiting for Zarkov to explain.

"Whatever caused the *Goodhope* to jump from Earth orbit brought us here. And it was not by chance. This planet evidently is home for the builders of the device that directed us here."

Dale shuddered. "I don't think much of their science. Unless they *always* land their vessels by crashing them."

Zarkov was shaking his head. "The *Goodhope* itself was falling apart. The device was a hyper drive unit and a Guardian computer wrapped in one, but all the ancillary systems were the *Goodhope's* design. The ship was simply not able to handle the strain. It fell apart."

Dale looked at her uncle with wonderment in her eyes. "You're actually glad we're here," she said accusingly. Harshly.

Zarkov reacted as if he had been slapped in the face. "Not under these circumstances," he said sadly.

Dale was instantly contrite and went into her uncle's arms. "I'm sorry . . . I'm sorry, uncle," she sobbed. "I didn't mean it."

"It's all right, my dear," Zarkov said, holding

his niece. "It will all work out. You'll see."

Flash turned away from Zarkov and Dale and looked toward the undergrowth. Something was out there. He was certain he had heard something beyond the dense green wall of vines and thick jungle brush. Something large. But the noise had stopped.

He strained to listen, but at first the only sounds he could hear besides Zarkov's clucking and Dale's sobbing were the fire on the shuttle craft and the rustling noise of the wind in the treetops far above them. But then it came again. Like something crashing through the underbrush. But at a distance.

Flash drew his laser pistol and turned back to Dale and Zarkov. "Let's head back toward the shuttle craft," he said, keeping his voice as calm and unhurried as possible.

Dale parted from her uncle and looked up at Flash, then back at the still burning shuttle craft. "Why?" she said. "There's nothing left of it."

"What is it, Flash?" Zarkov asked, reading the concern in Flash's eyes.

Again Flash heard the noise in the underbrush, but this time it was much closer, and Dale heard it as well. Her complexion went white and her eyes widened.

"Flash?" she said, drawing out the word.

"Let's go," Flash said, no longer hiding the urgency in his voice. He took Zarkov's arm and the three of them hurried back to the opening in the jungle that the crash landing had caused, coming as close to the burning craft as they could.

They turned to look back down the narrow alley

they had burned through the undergrowth in time to see the brush part and a gigantic beast, one that looked very much like the Earth bears they had seen in zoos and game preserves, only much larger, step onto the path. When it saw them, it raised up on its hind legs and bellowed.

Dale screamed and Flash raised his laser pistol, aimed directly at the center of the beast's chest, and as the creature began advancing toward them, he hit the firing stud. But nothing happened.

# CHAPTER 8

The bearlike creature, which stood at least four meters at the shoulders, dropped to all fours and charged them, bellowing and screaming as it lumbered out into the clearing. Flash threw down his totally discharged laser pistol, roughly shoved Zarkov back, and leapt forward, grabbing up a heavy branch from one of the downed trees.

There was little hope that he could more than slow the creature down, perhaps long enough to allow Dr. Zarkov and Dale to go around behind the still burning shuttle craft. It was possible that the beast was afraid of fire, like most wild animals, and would not attempt to pursue them.

The creature was almost on top of him, and he could smell its rank, fetid odor, but Flash was moving like a machine now as he stepped back, throwing his weight on his right foot and, holding the heavy branch like a club, began to swing it around. At the last second the beast rose up on its hind legs, its massive right paw coming at him like an express train, but then its head and most of its upper torso exploded in a wide blue streak that sent blood, bits of bone and flesh and fur flying everywhere. The forward momentum of the creature sent it toppling toward Flash, who at the last minute leapt to the left, rolling over twice, as the creature hit the ground and then lay still.

Flash turned slowly over and looked up in amazement at Dale, who stood less than a meter in front of what remained of the huge creature. She held her laser pistol on the dead animal in shaking hands, tears streaming down her cheeks, muttering and crying almost incoherently.

Zarkov started to move toward his niece when she began firing wildly at the creature in short bursts that blew holes in the animal's carcass, all the while screaming and shaking like a crazy woman.

Flash jumped up and coming up behind her grabbed her arms and pulled the weapon out of her hands. At first she tried to fight him, but then she collapsed in his arms, the tears coming freely.

"Oh God . . . God . . ." she cried, as Flash held her tight, crushing her tiny body against his with one arm as he handed the deadly pistol to a much shaken Zarkov with his other.

"It's all right now, Dale. It's all right. It's over now," Flash said, trying to calm her down.

Once before, during the trouble they had been involved with on Mars, Dale had saved his life, and later had collapsed in a fit of near hysteria. At that time he had been amazed at her ability to keep her head at least as long as the crises lasted. And now he was no less amazed with her. Only this time he felt something else for her. Something he had not felt for a woman for a very long time.

He continued holding her close, until at long last her tears began to subside, and she stopped shaking.

Finally she moved back from him and looked up into his eyes, her face streaked and dirty.

"I love you, Robert Gordon," she said softly. "No matter what you say or do, or how you feel about me, you must know that I love you and always will."

At that moment he wanted to pull her close to him and kiss her soft lips as something stirred deep within him; but then his wife's last cry for help and the sight of her broken body in their apartment intruded, and a blackness welled up from deep inside his gut, blotting out whatever it was he had almost felt for Dale, and he stepped back.

Dale smiled tiredly. "Your wife was a beautiful, wonderful woman. I know. And I know I could never replace her in your heart, or even come close to matching her. Nor could you ever feel for me what you felt for her."

Flash started to interrupt, but Dale reached up and silenced him with a finger on his lips. "No," she said gently, "don't say anything now that you might regret later. Just keep it in the back of your mind that I love you."

For a brief moment Flash knew that he was afraid. Terrified. He had loved deeply and had lost violently, and it had nearly killed him. He could not handle such a thing again.

He was about to explain that to Dale, when

Zarkov's strangled cry brought him instantly around.

A twin of the huge creature that Dale had killed had broken through the underbrush near the path they had cut, and stood on its hind legs looking at them. Flash moved slowly over to Zarkov and took the laser pistol from him, checking the charge. The weapon carried less than a quarter charge in its batteries, and was set on wide angle, the most power draining setting possible.

Another of the bearlike creatures came from the underbrush a meter away from the other creature, and in quick succession four more of the terrible beasts came out into the pathway.

Dale had come up behind him, and he herded her and Zarkov around the bow of the shuttle craft, putting the still burning vessel between them and the creatures.

"The fire has evidently attracted them," Zarkov said.

"Yes," Flash replied. "Let's hope that it will hold them from coming too close."

Two more of the beasts came crashing through the underbrush, and they began to slowly advance, snarling and bellowing, down the path.

Flash flipped the laser pistol onto narrow beam, got down on one knee and, steadying the weapon with both hands, fired a short burst at the lead animal, decapitating it in a blue flash.

The downed creature rolled and thrashed reflexively, and instantly the other beasts were on it, growling and screaming as they ripped the flesh from the dead animal's body and fought each other for the meat.

Three more of the creatures came crashing out of the underbrush from the left, and one came from the right. All of them charged the downed animal and soon the jungle was alive with their cries and screams.

"Now," Flash said urgently, and he led Dale and Zarkov away from the shuttle craft, keeping it between them and the feeding beasts.

At the edge of the clearing, Flash began cutting a path through the dense undergrowth, trying as best he could to conserve what little remained of the laser pistol's charge. Without it they would certainly not survive. But the jungle seemed to go on forever, and for a time Flash was convinced that there would be no way possible for them ever to make the seacoast, but then they came to the river.

It was a narrow, fast moving stream, not more than fifty meters across, with twists and turns, and in the center there were rocks and log jams around which the water gurgled in the waning light of the day. But the banks of the river were almost like a well tended park. From the jungle on either side of the river was a wide strip of low grass, with an occasional bush or small tree that sloped to a narrow shoreline of pale orange sand.

Across the river and downstream from them a small, deerlike animal was drinking, and when they emerged from the jungle it looked up, its wide, sad eyes studying them for a moment. Then it leisurely turned and gracefully disappeared into the dense jungle, leaving nothing more than an after-image in their eyes and wonder if they had ever really seen the lovely animal.

"This river almost certainly leads to the sea," Zarkov said.

The running water sparkled and shimmered in the lowering sunlight, and Flash shaded his eyes first upstream, and then turned to look downstream.

"It's running just a little south of east, unless this planet is on a large ecliptic with the sun."

"It's surprisingly near Earth normal," Zarkov said.

"Then the sun rises downstream, the east, which means that most likely the river does run into the sea."

Dr. Zarkov was completely worn out, and a large bruise had formed on his right cheek where he had struck his head in the crash landing of their shuttle craft. Dale was still shook up from the close call with the bearlike creatures, and Flash himself was bone tired.

He turned again to look upstream. The sun was near the horizon, and had turned a blood red color. It would be dark within a half hour, and none of them were in any condition to travel any farther this night.

He turned back to Dale and Zarkov. "We'll stay here tonight."

Dale looked nervously over her shoulder. "What about the animals?"

"I'll start a fire and we'll take turns sleeping. We can't continue now. It'll be dark soon."

Dale started to protest, but Zarkov cut her off. "He's right, Dale. I'm in no condition to go farther. We'll be all right here. We've got our pressure suits, and even without the helmets, they'll keep us warm and dry. There's plenty of water, and in the morning we'll head downstream."

"What about food?" she said in a small voice.

"You and your uncle can collect some firewood . . . I'll take care of the food," Flash said.

Zarkov nodded his agreement, and Flash turned and started downstream, but Dale gave out a little cry. "No . . . don't leave us."

Flash came back to her. "I'm not going far. In fact, I won't even be out of sight. I'm just going downstream a little ways and wait for some small animal to come to the water. At least we'll have meat."

She made a face, and Flash had to smile. "Don't tell me you're so used to autochef food that you don't remember what a good steak tastes like."

"A good steak, yes. The half-charred remains of some poor animal, cooked over a fire, I can do without."

"We'll see," Flash said, and he turned and headed along the riverbank downstream in a steady gait that in a few minutes took him several hundred meters away from where Dale and Zarkov had begun gathering wood and laying out a fire.

Flash set the laser pistol on the lowest possible setting and moved quietly away from the river so that he was hidden at the edge of the dense jungle foliage.

The only hunting he had ever done was on small game ranches in the forests of northern North America. But that had been several years ago. Since that time he had been too busy to indulge himself in the sport.

He had just settled down when two of the deer-like creatures they had seen on the other side of the

river came out of the jungle, evidently along a
game trail less than thirty meters from him. They
stopped at the edge of the clearing, seemed to sniff
the air, and then slowly trotted down to the river
bank where one drank as the other warily kept
watch.

Once, the animal looked directly at Flash, but it
either had poor eyesight or it did not consider
Flash to be a threat, because it turned to look the
other way.

The creatures were small, not much larger than a
dog, and one of them had a set of antlers, and was
probably the male.

Flash carefully aimed the laser pistol at the male
creature's side, where he thought its heart might
be, and squeezed off a short burst.

The animal jerked upright, startled, turned and
took several hesitant steps forward, then fell over
on its side. Its mate sprang immediately for the
protection of the jungle and was gone without a
glance backwards.

Flash slowly stood up and walked down into the
clearing and looked back. He could just barely
make out Dale's figure by the river, and a moment
later Zarkov came from the jungle.

He went downstream to the fallen animal. It had
a narrow hole burned completely through its torso
just behind the front shoulders. It was a sad looking creature, with large, dark eyes, and for a moment Flash felt a pang of guilt that he had killed it.
Yet he knew that he had had no choice. If they
were to survive on this planet they would need their
strength.

Carefully using the laser pistol, Flash field-
dressed the animal and cut several small steaks

from its hind quarters. They would be taking a risk
eating the meat, or drinking the water from the
river. All of it could be deadly poison to their systems. But they had no chem-analyzer, and would
have to trust to luck.

It was dark by the time Flash had hiked back
with the meat, started a fire with the now almost
completely discharged laser pistol, and put steaks
on sticks to roast.

The three of them sat hunched beside each other
by the fire, Dale in the middle, none of them saying
anything as they watched the fire. By the time the
meat had cooked, Zarkov seemed on the verge of
collapse, his complexion sallow, and from time to
time Dale glanced nervously over her shoulder toward the dark jungle.

The venison, which is what they called it for
want of a better name, was surprisingly tender and
mild, and tasted as if it had been seasoned with
lemon juice. Even Dale, who had earlier wanted no
part of eating the flesh of some poor creature, attacked her portion ravenously.

They all washed and drank from the cool, sweet
river, and Zarkov fell in a heap beside the fire,
asleep within moments after he made Flash promise to wake him when it was his turn to stand
guard.

The smells and night sounds of this planet were
very little different than those in any Earth jungle,
and the lulling sound of the gurgling river, the
crackling of the camp fire, and the feeling of well-
being after eating all made Dale drowsy. She
stretched out by the fire and laid her head on
Flash's lap.

For a long time neither of them said anything, and Flash suspected Dale had fallen asleep, her eyes were closed and her breathing regular. But she smiled after awhile, moved a little closer to the fire, and then opened her eyes and looked up at Flash.

"Go to sleep," he said gently. "I'll wake you when it's your turn to stand guard."

"You know you're going to end up marrying me," she said.

Flash said nothing, his gut tightening.

"I mean, if we're really stuck on this planet with no way home, we'll have to do our best to populate the place."

Flash could not decide whether or not she was joking with him. "You've got this all figured out, I see."

She sat up. "Seriously, what do you and Uncle Hans expect to find tomorrow on the seacoast?"

"I don't know," Flash said carefully. He did not want to build up any false hopes in her. "Perhaps nothing but the ocean."

"But perhaps something besides the ocean," she insisted. "What's that *something?*"

"Your uncle explained it," Flash said. "The machine or device or whatever it was in the *Goodhope*'s drive room brought us here without any help from us. Which means there's a good likelihood that its designers and builders inhabit this place."

"We were the intruders. Perhaps this is a prison world we were sent to."

"Perhaps," Flash said noncommittally. He could see that Dale was working herself up again. He had not told her or her uncle exactly how low their remaining laser pistol charge had fallen. But at this moment he doubted if there was enough

power left in the weapon to down another deer
animal, let alone stop or even seriously slow down
one of the bear creatures. The seacoast would provide them a certain safety away from the jungle. If
they could make it that far.

Dale laid her head back in Flash's lap and closed
her eyes. "Who do you suppose killed the crew and
passengers?" she asked, her voice dreamy. "The
missing woman?"

"I think so," Flash answered. "She probably
went insane, killed them all in their sleep, and
went out an airlock without her suit."

"But why?"

"We'll probably never know."

Dale muttered something else that Flash could
not quite catch, and then she was alseep.

Flash watched her sleep for a half hour or so, but
then he gently moved her head from his lap, got up
and stretched, and laid some more wood on the
fire.

The night was mild, and the wind had shifted to
the east. Over the musky smells of the jungle he
was sure he could smell the fresh, clean odor of the
sea, and he asked himself the same question Dale
had asked. What *did* they expect to find tomorrow
on the seacoast? Merely safety? Or were they really
expecting friendly natives in grass huts, like the
ones Flash remembered from his history lessons?
They were near the planet's equator, so they were
in the tropical region much like Earth's equatorial
South America or Africa. Or did they expect
to find signs of a civilization advanced enough to
have built the hyper drive device that had brought
them here? If that was the case, the *Goodhope's*
crash would have been detected, as would the

launching and crash landing of the shuttle craft. Long before now there should have been a search party of some kind out here looking for them.

Something else was bothering Flash as well, however. It had bothered him while they were still aboard the *Goodhope,* and despite his efforts during that week, he had not come up with a satisfactory answer. It was the young woman missing from the cryo station. According to the *Goodhope*'s design, and computer taped logs, several of the crew members were automatically awakened at long intervals. *Several* crew members, not one lone female passenger.

What was the woman doing awake? Had there been a malfunction in the equipment that brought her out of deep sleep ahead of the others? Or was it something else. . . ?

He looked across the fire at Dale's sleeping figure. Most likely she would get her wish, if that's what it was, and they would have to begin populating this planet. Perhaps they could find some usable equipment from the *Goodhope*'s remains to increase the power of their suit radios making them distress beacons. But even with that they would have to expect to remain the rest of their lives here.

Some creature screamed in the jungle, but it was a long distance away, and Flash moved quietly back to the fire and wearily sat down next to Dale to wait for the morning.

The sun was shining directly upriver when Flash awoke with a start. For a moment he was totally disoriented, not knowing where he was, but then it all came back to him, and he sat up.

Zarkov was still sleeping by the smoldering remains of their camp fire, and a moment later Flash spotted Dale by the river. She had taken off her pressure suit, and was just stepping out of her coveralls as he stood up. The morning was warm, the air rich and incredibly sweet on a light breeze. The slightly less than Earth gravity, combined with a higher oxygen content in the atmosphere, made recovery from any physical ordeal much quicker to a person accustomed to Earth normal conditions. Flash felt good, forgetting for at least the first few moments the predicament they were in as he watched Dale, nude, step into the water, her back to him. She was slightly upstream, and had found a pool formed by a log jam caught against a line of rocks. She waded farther out into the pool until the water became deep enough for her to swim, then kicked off, gliding gracefully toward the log jam.

Flash took off his bulky pressure suit and laid it down beside the fire. Stuffing the laser pistol into a leg pocket of his coveralls, he went down to the river, splashed some water on his face, then walked upstream to where Dale was swimming.

She was not aware that he was standing on shore watching her, and when she reached the log jam she started to climb up on it.

"Are you sure you want to climb up there?" Flash said.

Dale spun around, splashing back into the water, and for a moment she glared at him, but then she smiled and began swimming back toward shore.

"I've never played Tri-V with you, Colonel Gordon, so I've never had the pleasure of sharing a locker room with you," she called as she swam.

"But if you remain standing where you are, the effect will be the same when I reach shore."

Flash laughed, reached down and picked up her coveralls where she had dropped them, and threw them over his shoulder, "Why didn't you wake me when you got up?"

She had stopped swimming and was treading water in the middle of the pool, a horrified expression on her face.

Flash laughed even louder. "I won't steal your clothes . . ." he started to say, but Dale was gesturing wildly at something behind him, farther upstream.

He turned in time to see a pair of the bear creatures coming around the bend of the river on their side of the shore. They were still several hundred meters away, but even at this distance they looked huge and menacing.

"Get out of the water, now," Flash said in a level voice, throwing down her coveralls. "I'll get your uncle."

Dale headed for shore, her powerful strokes slicing cleanly through the water, as Flash hurried back to the campsite to wake Zarkov.

The old man woke instantly. "Is it my watch?"

"We've got troubles," Flash said, and he helped Zarkov to his feet and pointed upstream.

Dale had reached shore, and was pulling on her coveralls as the beasts spotted her, and came lumbering slowly downstream.

Dale saw them coming, and headed in a dead run back to the camp, zippering up her clothes as she ran.

Flash turned and quickly helped Zarkov out of his confining pressure suit, and by the time they

had it off, Dale had reached them. Together they
headed downstream, the bear creatures following
them at a leisurely pace.

Within a couple of minutes they had passed the
spot where yesterday afternoon Flash had killed
the deerlike animal, but nothing remained of the
animal's carcass except for a path flattened
through the grass where some night creature had
evidently dragged it off.

And then they were around another slight bend
in the river, and out of sight of the beasts pursuing
them.

For nearly an hour they kept up a steady pace,
never again sighting the bear creatures behind
them, but finally Zarkov began to seriously tire,
and they had to stop.

They sat in the sand by the river, and Zarkov lay
back, his eyes closed, his breathing rapid. They
would have to slow down, Flash figured, or Zarkov
would never make it all the way to the sea.

The morning sun had come well up into the sky
and Flash squinted up at it, roughly estimating its
angular height above the horizon, and then he
looked at his chronometer strapped to his wrist.

Zarkov had opened his eyes and was watching
him. "What does it work out to be, Flash?" he
said, wheezing.

"With the rate the sun is coming up, I'd say the
rotational period is probably right around twenty-
two hours, perhaps a little less."

"So we have less daylight to reach the seacoast
and explore than we first expected."

"It would appear so," Flash said.

"Uncle Hans can't go on like this much longer,"
Dale said.

Zarkov sat up, took a deep breath, and managed a slight smile. "I'd rather be a worn out old man than breakfast for the bears behind us."

Dale looked sharply at Flash. "Are they still following us?"

Flash looked back upstream. "We'll wait here while you run upstream to take a look," he said lightly. The worst possible thing that could happen to them would be if they panicked. He had watched others learn that lesson painfully. Keep it light, the Federation CID manual cautioned.

"You're impossible," Dale snapped.

Flash turned back to her. "And you're quite lovely with your clothes off."

She reddened, but said nothing, and Zarkov laughed. "You'll have to teach me how to do that, Flash," he said. "I've never been able to get the last word in with her."

"You're as bad as he is, uncle," Dale said, but she too had to laugh, the ominous mood broken.

Flash got to his feet and helped Zarkov up. "How do you feel, doc? Can you go on?"

Zarkov nodded. "But let's slow it down a bit. I don't want to end up having to be carried."

"Sure," Flash said, and without another glance upstream, the three of them continued east, walking through the low grass in a slow but steady pace as the sun continued to climb toward its zenith in the morning sky.

Through the remainder of the morning they saw no further signs of the bear creatures behind them, and around noon they found a tree growing near the jungle's edge that was laden with a pale green fruit shaped much like a pear.

They stopped and Zarkov plucked one of them

off the tree, crushed it open, sniffed the juice, and touched his fingers to his lips.

"Tastes like a cross between an orange and maybe a grapefruit," he said. And before they could stop him he took a large bite of it, chewed it thoughtfully, and then swallowed it.

"Uncle!" Dale cried, and she grabbed the pear from his hands and threw it away.

He smiled. "Someone had to try it," he said, and he turned to Flash. "Let's take some of these along with us. If after a half hour I'm not flat on my back, it should be safe to eat one or two of them."

"That was a foolish thing to do," Flash said.

"I know, but are there any other alternatives?"

"No," Flash said softly after a moment. He thought about the risks they had already taken with the "deer" meat and the river water. It could not be helped if they wanted any chance at all of survival.

They pulled several of the pears off the tree, stuffed them in their coverall pockets, and continued downstream, the day turning warm under a pale blue sky.

Around one o'clock, apparent time, Zarkov pulled one of the pears from his pocket and began eating it, and, after a moment, Dale and Flash followed suit. The fruit was delicious, with only a slight, pleasant tang to it, and after they had eaten a couple of them, they felt refreshed and were able to pick up the pace a bit.

It was late in the day by the time they stopped again. Zarkov was worn out and he sank down gratefully on the narrow strip of sand by the water's edge. Immediately, however, all of them noticed that something was different.

Flash was staring at the river, and Dale had cocked her head and was listening to something. They both turned toward each other at the same time.

"The river," Flash said getting to his feet. "It's running faster."

"Listen to that sound," Dale said, and she too jumped to her feet.

And then they all could hear it—a dull rushing noise, like a heavy wind in the treetops, only at a great distance.

"It's a waterfall," Flash said, taking a couple of steps forward. "And it has to be right on the coast. We've come far enough for that."

Zarkov painfully got to his feet. "What are we waiting for then?"

"You're in no shape to continue . . ." Flash started to say but the old scientist cut him off.

"I'll do my resting much easier once we get there, and away from this jungle. It can't be too far now."

"Are you sure, doc?" Flash asked. He was concerned for his friend. They had come this far relatively unscathed. He didn't want anything to happen to the old man now. "We can rest here for a half hour or so, then continue. There's plenty of light left."

Zarkov was shaking his head. "We'll just take it easy, that's all. I want to get away from this jungle."

They started out again, working their way slowly downstream, the noise of the waterfall growing louder the farther they went, until a half an hour later they could see the mist of the falling water rising up ahead of them, and the jungle fell away

on either side of the river, revealing a fore-
shortened horizon. The closer they came to the apparent land's end, the more it became clear that
they were on some kind of a plateau, and Dale, no
longer able to contain herself, sprinted forward the
last couple of hundred meters.

The noise of the falling water was very loud now,
and Zarkov had to shout to be heard over its roar.
"She is a wonderful girl, Flash. She has been like a
daughter to me."

Flash was helping the old man limp along, sup-
porting most of his weight with an arm around his
waist. He turned to look down at his friend and
teacher. "She has it in her head that she's in love
with me."

Zarkov looked up at Flash, a shrewd, knowing
expression in his eyes. "She's loved you from the
first time she met you. Even before your wife's
death."

Flash said nothing.

"If it happens that we must remain here . . ."
Zarkov started with much difficulty, and then he
hesitated. "If it happens, treat her well."

"Yes," Flash said, feeling somewhat foolish that
he could think of nothing else to say.

Dale screamed, and both men snapped that way.
She was a couple of hundred meters downstream,
and she was standing perfectly still.

They both began running as fast as they could,
Flash breaking away from Zarkov and pulling far
ahead. He shouted her name, but she did not move,
nor did she utter another sound. As he ran, Flash
pulled the laser pistol out of his pocket and set it on
maximum power. He would only have one shot,
and would have to be careful to make it count.

Flash raced to Dale's side. She was standing near the edge of a sheer cliff that dropped perhaps three hundred meters to the sea, which stretched east as far as they could see, meeting the horizon in the hazy distance.

Dale was staring speechless to the northeast, and Flash followed her gaze. The sight stunned him, nearly causing his mind to go completely blank.

They were at the edge of a large cove, the river ending in a waterfall, slightly south of the middle. To the north, on the opposite side of the cove, and stretching as far as they could see, was what appeared to be a city, but a city the likes of which Flash had never seen.

Spires of every imaginable color shimmered in the sunlight almost like a mirage seen at the end of a rainbow; large arched structures, and huge curved buildings that had to be several kilometers on a side were visible from here. What appeared to be wharves and docks along the edge of the sea were lined up in absolute perfection. Elevated roads and bridges interlaced the taller buildings. The sheer beauty of the vision took their breath away—as did the realization that the existence of such a magnificent city meant they were not alone on this planet, and that whoever built it would surely have the technology to allow them to return home.

Zarkov had finally reached them, and when he too saw the city in the distance, his eyes watered and he shook his head in wonder.

"My God," he said softly. "My God."

# CHAPTER 9

It was dark by the time Flash had managed to shoot a small, rabbitlike creature that had come to the river upstream to drink, and they had started a camp fire near the edge of the cliff well away from the waterfall. But none of them had paid much attention to the scanty meal, as they speechlessly watched the city come alive in the distance.

Lights first began coming on deep within the bowels of the city, illuminating the entire horizon with a soft, rosy glow. Then lights in the towers began to wink on, one at a time, it seemed, and almost religious in its beauty.

A light breeze had sprung up, making the camp fire dance and flicker. Dale sat to one side of the fire, her knees hunched up to her chin as she stared across the bay at the magnificent sight in the distance. She was entranced, and for the first time since the *Goodhope* had suddenly left Earth orbit, she seemed relaxed and no longer frightened.

Zarkov, however, who had been just as intent in his study of the city, seemed strangely troubled.

Flash had left the camp fire and had gone down to the river to wash up, and Zarkov got wearily to his feet and followed him. They were fifty meters or so away from where Dale was sitting, still staring at the city, and they were completely out of her earshot. Yet Zarkov kept his voice low.

"I didn't want to say anything in front of Dale— her hopes are already too high," the old man said without preamble.

Flash, who had gotten down on his knees in the sand to scoop water from the river with his cupped hands, looked up, and then got to his feet. Zarkov was definitely worried.

"What is it, doc?"

The light was dim, the flickering flames from the camp fire a long way off, but Flash could see the grim expression on Zarkov's features.

"Have you noticed anything strange about the city?"

From where they stood they could see the taller spires across the bay, and Flash glanced that way. "What do you mean?" he asked, keeping his voice low like the doctor's.

"I've been watching it since we first saw it, and I've been able to detect no activity other than the lights coming on at dark."

"We're too far away . . ." Flash started to protest, but Zarkov shook his head.

"We're not too far away to see ships coming in from the sea. Those are docks and warehouses down there, with no activity. We're not too far away to see atmospheric vessels, or at least the aircraft's lights. We're also not too far away to see traffic moving in the city."

Again Flash looked toward the city, and for a long time both men stared across the bay, saying nothing to each other.

"Nothing," Flash said finally. He turned back to Zarkov. "But that doesn't necessarily mean the city's dead. Perhaps the dock workers are on strike. Perhaps it's a national holiday," he said, but even as he spoke he knew he was grasping at straws.

Zarkov was shaking his head sadly. "Some central switching mechanism is turning on the lights. Perhaps sending out radio beacons. Running at least some of the functions of the city."

"Where are the people?"

Zarkov shrugged. "Plague. War. We won't know until we get down there tomorrow. And perhaps we'll never know."

"I thought it strange when I first saw the city that there had been no search and rescue parties out looking for us. Whoever built that place surely detected the *Goodhope*'s crash, and the launching of the shuttle craft. *If* they're there."

"Yes," Zarkov said, chewing thoughtfully on his lower lip. "And yet if we assume the city is dead, its population gone, we run into another problem that does not fit the facts."

"The unit aboard the *Goodhope*," Flash said.

"Exactly. Who put it there and why did it bring us here?"

Dale had come up behind them, and stood a couple of meters away in the darkness. She was shivering. "There's no one alive down there, is there?"

Flash and Zarkov spun around at the sound of her voice, but she made no move to come closer.

"We don't know that, my dear," Zarkov said, but there was no conviction in his voice.

"Yes, you do," Dale said, her voice rising. She half turned to glance at the city. "There's no one alive down there. They're all dead or gone someplace. We're still alone."

Flash started toward her. "Even if the people are all gone, there is the city," he said.

"No," she cried, and she turned and ran back to the fire.

Flash was going to follow her, but Zarkov stopped him. "Leave her be for a while," he said.

"She needs someone to tell her everything will be all right."

Zarkov looked into Flash's eyes. "Are you going to lie to her?" he said firmly, and when Flash said nothing he shook his head. "That wouldn't help. She's a strong woman, and she's going to have to work this out for herself. When she accepts the fact that we're truly alone here, she'll be an asset instead of a liability."

Flash was surprised to hear Zarkov talk that way, and he said so, but Zarkov overrode him.

"We're talking now about survival, Flash," he said. "You're banking too heavily on finding something to help us in the city. Perhaps we will find something. But perhaps the technology will be so incomprehensible to us, there'll be nothing for us to use." He turned and together they headed slowly back to the camp fire, where Dale was again seated, her knees hunched up, staring out across the bay at the city.

"We'll also be running the risk that the city could be dangerous to us. It would be like transporting an early Earth savage to New Los Angeles. The man would not last a day. He'd be run down by traffic, perhaps electrocuted, perhaps he'd step in the way of a laser guidance system and be blown apart, or perhaps he'd step the wrong way into a grav tube and fall to his death. There'd be a million and one dangers because of his lack of knowledge and comprehension of our technology. The same could hold true for us tomorrow down in the city."

"Are you telling me that we should stay away?" Flash asked.

"No," Zarkov said intensely. "I am saying, however, that we must be exceedingly careful, and that you must not count too heavily on finding something to help us."

"If worse comes to worse, we've got the rest of our lives to figure out at least the communications capabilities of the city."

"No, Flash," Zarkov said. "Our ignorant savage brought to a deserted but still functioning New Los Angeles, would never in several lifetimes figure out the principles of electricity, let alone deep space communications, or something so common as molecular bonding. But he might very well die in any attempt to fiddle with unknown technologies."

"We have one up on the savage, though," Flash continued to argue. "And that is we understand the concept of a library, or a computer information system. We can learn."

"Perhaps," Zarkov said. "Perhaps." But he did not sound convinced.

Dale had recovered, somewhat, from her outburst by the river, and when Flash and Zarkov reached the fire and sat down, she looked up and managed a slight smile.

"How are you feeling now?" Zarkov asked his niece solicitously.

"Much better, uncle," she said. "I'm sorry I lost my head. I don't know what got into me."

"You're tired. We've come a long way today," he said.

"Are we going down there tomorrow?" she asked.

Zarkov nodded. "Yes."

Her smile broadened. "Good," she said. "That means tomorrow night I'll be able to sleep in a bed, instead of on the ground."

Flash said nothing, but he and Zarkov exchanged glances, and within a few minutes, they had all settled down for the night.

Zarkov took the first watch, and when he saw the nearly totally discharged level of the laser pistol's battery indicator, he added a couple more logs to the fire.

The night, like the previous day, passed quickly, and by morning all of them were hungry, but decided not to hunt for meat, satisfying their hunger instead with the remainder of the pears they had picked from the fruit tree upstream yesterday.

A couple of kilometers upstream they had passed an area in which the river had widened considerably. There, the water was not so fast moving, nor had it looked too deep.

They hiked back up to that spot at first light, reaching the area in about a half an hour. Flash waded across the river first, and although the current was somewhat more swift than he had thought it would be, the water never got deeper than waist high, and within a couple of minutes they all were safely on the opposite shore and had started back to the sea.

The morning was pleasantly warm, the sky clear, and the breeze, as they came to the cliff, was light and smelling sweetly of the sea. Although they saw several small animals, including one herd of at least a dozen of the deerlike animals, they encountered none of the bear creatures.

At the cliff they headed north, the land gently sloping down and slightly to the east, toward a wide sand beach far below them.

As they walked through the low grass a few meters away from the cliff's edge, Dale's spirits seemed much improved over last night's, and she hummed several of the tunes that had been popular on Earth before they had left.

Zarkov, too, seemed in much better condition than he had yesterday, despite the facts that they had not eaten much, and had been forced into sleeping out in the open.

Flash supposed it was a combination of the lesser gravity and higher oxygen, because he felt good; the gloom that had pervaded their spirits last night had evaporated with the morning sun.

It was around apparent noon by the time they reached the beach and discovered the highway—and with it the certainty that the city, now less than five kilometers distant, was deserted.

The road angled in toward the sea from the west, then curved north, directly into the city a few hundred meters up from the beach.

Flash had spotted it first as an unnatural flatness in the terrain from where they were approaching the city, and the three of them clambered up a steep slope and walked out onto the wide roadway.

The highway was surfaced with a material that none of them had ever seen before. It seemed somehow like a combination of materials—solid rock with an impenetrable plastic overlay that felt to the touch like slick glass. It was not pitted, scarred, or in any way weathered, but for as far as they could see in either direction it was littered with leaves, fallen branches, and animal droppings.

"This road hasn't been used in a hundred years or more," Zarkov said, gazing toward the city. At this distance the spires towered high above them, the tallest ones rising certainly a thousand meters or more.

"The place is deserted after all," Dale said softly. She turned and looked back the way they had come, the waterfall spectacularly falling from the high cliffs down into a huge pool that ran into the sea. A rainbow shimmered in the rising mist halfway down the cliff.

"We have a decision to make," Zarkov said. Dale turned back to face him. "Back there by the river we have water, and with fruit, perhaps berries, and whatever small game we can manage to catch, we have food. But ahead, in the city, we might find nothing. No food or water."

"What are you saying, uncle?" Dale said, a sharp note in her voice.

"I'm saying it might be wiser for us to go back up the beach to the base of the waterfall where

there is fresh water. Perhaps we can find some
shellfish or some other food. When we've eaten
and spent another night of rest, we can go into the
city at first light."

Dale was shaking her head. "No," she said flat-
ly. "I don't want to spend another night in the
open. If some mechanism is turning on the lights at
night, surely there must be at least fresh water running. We can find it."

"Flash?" Zarkov said, turning away from his
niece.

"If we find nothing in the city I can always hike
up the beach to the waterfall and bring some water
back. I'm sure we'd be able to find at least some
kind of container. I think we should go on." He
looked down the road toward the city. "One way
or another, our survival here is going to depend
pretty heavily on what we find or don't find in the
city. The sooner we start looking, the sooner we
can get on with it."

Zarkov nodded his agreement with some reser-
vation, and they headed down the littered road into
the city, each of them with their own expectations
and fears, but all of them understanding that this
was not just a pleasant afternoon's walk in the
countryside; it was a matter of life and death.

The highway followed the slight contour of the
beach to their right, aiming directly toward the
area of wharves and docks. As they got closer they
could distinguish several wide buildings that obviously had been used as warehouses.

Nowhere else, however, did they see other high-
ways, as would be expected to lead into a city of
this large size if ground transportation were the

principle means of travel. They also began to see, the closer they got, that the city was actually constructed on two levels. The lower level, which was what they were on, contained the highway, which led to the docks, warehouses, and a series of dark openings beneath the buildings. The streets, if there were any, and the building entrances were at a higher level, about ten meters above the highway. Nowhere that they could see were there stairs, ramps, or any other normal means of getting to the upper level. At least, not at the city's edge.

By early afternoon, they had trudged across a low bridge over what appeared to be a tidal flat, and they were in the city, or at least in the city's waterfront district. The highway continued straight along the docks, the warehouse buildings on the sea side and the tunnels beneath the city's buildings on the inland side.

The buildings at this level, like the roadway, were constructed of a material that looked like living rock, but shimmered in the sun, and to the touch felt like glass. And, like the road, none of the warehouse buildings showed any sign of age or weathering other than the droppings of animals and birds, and the grass, leaves, and branches that had blown in along the highway.

At the entrance to the tunnels leading beneath the city was a thick layer of dust in areas protected from the wind. It had been a very long time indeed since anyone had been here.

None of the warehouses seemed to have any entrances, but instead looked like nothing more than huge, shaped chunks of plastic covered rock. In some respects it seemed as if the warehouses had

been carved from a layer of rock and were really
nothing more than elaborate sculptures.

About two kilometers along the warehouse road
they came finally to a wide ramp that led upward at
a steep angle to the city level. It was Dale who first
noticed the obvious difference between the ramp
and the roadway along which they had been trav-
eling.

"It's clean," she gasped, looking up the ramp.

For a moment Flash did not understand what
she was trying to say, but then it hit him. The ramp
was *clean.* It had obviously been used, and recently, because unlike the roadway there was no debris,
and its surface gleamed in the sunlight almost as if
it had been polished today.

Dale started up the ramp, running as fast as her
legs would carry her, and Zarkov shouted for her
to wait, but it was too late; she either did not hear
him or chose to ignore his warning, because she did
not stop until she topped the rise, and then she uttered a little cry of what sounded like delight.

Flash and Zarkov hurried up behind her, and by
the time they got to the top of the ramp the old
scientist was winded, but the sight that greeted
them made him gasp.

The three of them stood gape-mouthed at the
head of the ramp, staring down a wide, tree-lined
boulevard. That the throughway had been used ex-
clusively for foot traffic and not for vehicles of any
kind was obvious from the wide, bricked footpaths
meandering seemingly at random through well-
tended grass, shrubbery, small trees, and flowers.
Here and there were elaborately carved fountains
spewing fantastically shaped sprays of water; small

animals grazed amidst a riot of a thousand shades of green mixed with a virtual rainbow of colors in the fountains, the flowers, and the walkways themselves. It seemed to be a cross between a well-kept zoo or animal park, a nature preserve, and a place of obvious human habitation.

On either side of the wide mall, which stretched ahead as far as they could see, were the fabulous buildings of the city, including the huge, but graceful, spires that shimmered and twinkled in the sunlight.

At street level, if it could be called that, the buildings were glass-fronted, and behind the wide windows were a riot of goods and many totally incomprehensible things. They obviously were in a shopping district, and Dale was beside herself with joy and excitement.

Flash and Zarkov, however, realized the import of what they were seeing almost immediately. The grass had been recently clipped; the storefront windows had been cleaned; and despite the small animals running through the low bushes and hedges, the walkways were spotlessly shined. The city was *not* deserted.

Dale started forward along a walkway that led toward the storefronts, but Flash stopped her.

"I think we'd better be careful," he said.

She did a pirouette out of his grasp and ran skipping down the path. "It's glorious," she cried, her voice echoing off the buildings. "It's wonderful!"

Zarkov was the first to see a movement along the walkway directly in front of the stores, and he shouted his warning.

Dale stopped in mid-stride and half turned back,

an uncertain expression on her face. "Uncle . . ." she started to say, but then she too saw it.

A couple of hundred meters away, but moving toward them rapidly, was some kind of a small, robotic-controlled vehicle riding on an air or anti-grav cushion. It was a dull gray in color and made absolutely no sound as it glided down the pathway.

Dale started toward Flash and Zarkov, and the machine, sensing her movement, angled down another path directly toward her.

Flash leapt forward and raced toward Dale as large claws extended from the front of the vehicle, and it sped up.

The machine was narrow, and just behind what apparently was the control and sensory apparatus was a tall, open bin.

At the last moment, the vehicle almost on top of Dale, Flash leapt into the air, kicking out with both of his feet, slamming into the side of the machine, knocking it over with a crash.

Dale had jumped back, and when Flash got to his feet he grabbed her roughly by the elbow and raced back toward the ramp, as the machine he had knocked over, claws snapping, tried to right itself, much like a turtle trying to rock itself back to its feet after being knocked over.

Zarkov shouted another warning, and Flash looked up in time to see at least a half dozen of the little machines converging on them and the downed vehicle, cutting off any hope of escape to the ramp.

# CHAPTER 10

Flash, still hauling Dale with him, angled away from the machines that were headed toward the ramp entrance, crossed one of the walkways, rushed across a wide lawn, and crashed into a line of well-tended bushes. A moment later a white-faced, almost completely winded Zarkov joined them.

"If we can make it to one of the fountains I don't think the machines will follow us into the water," Flash shouted. He was worried about Dr. Zarkov, and did not think the old man could take much more of this. If he collapsed now it would be almost impossible to save him against such stiff odds.

But Zarkov was catching his breath, and managed a slight smile. "Never mind, Flash," he said between gasps. "I think we'll be safe here."

"Those things . . ." Dale started to cry, her entire body shivering, but Zarkov placed a hand on her shoulder.

"Look," he said gently.

Flash, who had been ready to bolt at the first sign that the machines were coming into the bushes after them, bodily carrying both Zarkov and Dale if need be, followed Zarkov's direction, and he too suddenly realized what was happening.

Two of the machines had pulled the downed vehicle upright and were towing it away, while a half dozen other machines were cleaning and polishing the walkways, paying absolutely no further attention to anything outside their tasks.

Zarkov caught his breath, then pushed out from the hedgerow. Breaking off a branch from one of the bushes, he moved over to one of the walkways and threw it down on the pavement.

Instantly one of the machines glided over to within a meter of the unmoving Zarkov, scooped up the bit of debris, and then turned away.

Zarkov laughed out loud. "Janitors," he said, turning back to Dale and Flash.

"Janitors?" Dale asked incredulously as she and Flash came out of the bushes.

Zarkov was nodding and laughing even harder. For a moment Flash was certain that the old man was having an hysterical reaction to the stress of a few moments ago. But once again Zarkov regained his composure.

"We didn't belong here, so the machines interpreted us as debris . . . as trash . . . and came out to remove us. When we attacked one of their kind, more came out to repair the damage and clean up the mess."

"The bins on the back are for trash," Dale said, gazing with wonder at several of the machines still busy on cleanup detail.

"Which is fine—except for two things," Flash said. "The first is the trash they pick up. I'm sure they destroy it somewhere. Which means if we're picked up, we're dead."

Dale shuddered, but Zarkov was looking directly into Flash's eyes.

"The technology is the second thing that has you bothered, isn't it," Zarkov said, and Flash nodded.

"They don't fit, doc. Unless I miss my guess, I'd say they were made of some kind of old-fashioned aluminum alloy. Quite a long way, technologically, from the drive unit aboard the *Goodhope* and this city."

"Perhaps we're in a museum," Dale suggested.

"No," Zarkov said thoughtfully. "Flash is correct. I'd guess that the janitors were built and put here long after this city was deserted."

"By whom?" Dale said, the words catching in her throat.

"I don't know," Zarkov said slowly. He turned to watch as the last of the janitor robots departed the way they had come, leaving behind a spotlessly clean mall. "But I think if we can discover who did build them, and why, we might be a long way toward figuring out why this city was deserted."

"If it is," Flash said, and both Zarkov and Dale turned to look at him.

"What do you mean, Flash?" Zarkov asked, after a long moment of silence.

"I don't know," Flash said carefully. "Just a feeling, I guess." He looked across the mall at the storefront windows with their myriads of goods, and then gazed down the long, gaily colored canyon between the huge buildings.

Whoever constructed this city had to have been

very close to human. The entire feeling of the place was one of comfort, and more important, familiarity. It was as if he had been here before. And yet he certainly had not been here before, nor had he ever been to a place even remotely resembling this one. Yet the feeling almost of *déjà vu* was strong.

"I'm not going back to the river," Dale said, trying to be firm but not doing a very good job of it.

Flash turned to her. "No, we're not going back. For better or worse, our survival is still dependent upon what we find here."

"Which leaves us two choices and a couple of necessities," Zarkov said. "We can either camp right here until morning, or continue exploring until we find something in one of the shops that we can use."

"And the necessities?" Flash asked.

"Water we've got from the fountains in abundance. But we still need food and shelter."

"There's not enough power in the laser pistol to bring down even a small animal, or probably enough to start a fire. And I don't relish the idea of trying to chase down one of the animals we've seen here, and eat it raw. That leaves the shops."

"If I find a dress that fits, I'll shoplift it, and wear it tonight," Dale said flippantly, and her comment served to lighten their mood.

"It took the janitor robots awhile to come out after we intruded, so if we keep off the walkways, only crossing them when necessary, we should be all right," Zarkov said as they set off.

The three of them headed across the wide lawn toward the nearest line of shops as the sun lowered in the sky. Soon it would be dark, and Flash wanted to find shelter and food long before that. He did not relish the idea of spending another night in the open, especially without a fire, and he did not think Dale or Zarkov would fare too well without food or shelter.

The first dozen shops they looked at contained nothing in their windows that was comprehensible to them. In one shop the window display contained what appeared to be bolts of material, in another there were small devices with blank screens that could have been anything from miniature holograph recorder-viewers to pocket-sized Guardians. In still another shop window there were displayed at least a hundred oddly shaped blocks of what appeared to be rocks of some kind.

Everything they saw was tantalizingly familiar, and yet strange, and as the sun started setting Flash began to wonder if they would not have been better off remaining another night at the base of the waterfall as Dr. Zarkov had suggested. At least they would have been assured of some kind of food.

Zarkov was the first to feel the uneasiness, and he turned to look over his shoulder. They stood in the lee of a large spire, the base of which jutted several meters out into the mall. The setting sun cast long shadows from the building's edge, and Zarkov moved away from the shop window almost as if he were being magnetically drawn forward.

A moment later Dale looked up and followed her uncle, and then Flash felt it.

The best he could have described the sudden feeling that came over him was that his entire body was a musical instrument string, and that someone,

or something, was strumming it. He too turned and
followed Zarkov and Dale out into the mall to face
the setting sun. Coming over the horizon was a
sight that at once frightened and comforted him.

A rainbow seemed to shoot across the sky above
the sun, accompanied by a deep, subaudible rumbling: the effect was jarring, unsettling. But within
several seconds the area beneath the vivid arc of
color began to fill in with a swirling, almost blind-
ing pattern of colors and flashes of lights, all accompanied by tones, almost musical, but still subaudible.

Soft lights began coming on all along the mall,
illuminating the water fountains in a kaleidoscope
of colors; and still the thing that took up half the
western horizon seemed to grow and undulate,
changing subtly from a two-dimensional scene
against the backdrop of the sky, into a three-
dimensional thing of infinite beauty.

Flash felt himself being drawn west down the
mall behind Zarkov and Dale, moving against his
will, and yet not resisting, heedless of where they
were going as they stepped off the grass and
worked their way past the storefronts down a wide,
gold-colored walkway.

Flash was only dimly aware that other lights
were coming on above and around him, as he was
only vaguely aware of the passage of time until
they came to the globe near the stairs, and a wave
of euphoria swept through him like a wind through
a field of natural wheat.

Overlapping visions seemed to cross his mind's
eye—making love with his wife, with Dale; talking
with Dr. Zarkov; flying the *Intrepid*; winning a Tri-V

match; drinking a fine wine; wind sailing in the South Pacific—all of that with an overlying feeling of well-being that sent his entire soul craving for more, like the smell of a delicately scented flower that is hard to detect, and yet definitely there.

And he felt power, and knowledge, and freedom ... so much so that he could look at Dale and Zarkov, strangely far below him, with sympathy that they did not understand as he did what was happening.

All those feelings were real, to the point that Flash had the feeling he was experiencing all the pleasures he had ever felt in his life over again. Yet still another portion of his brain was acknowledging the fact that the three of them were standing beneath a huge, clear globe made of some kind of plastic; it hovered over the entrance to a set of wide stairs that led downward to a brightly lit corridor below.

The vision on the western horizon began to intensify, not only in color but in the rapidity of its changes. As the images began to race and flow in no recognizable patterns through Flash's brain, he began to feel pain—a searing, stabbing agony that cut through his gut.

Dale had sunk to her knees and Zarkov was on the verge of toppling over, when something distracted Flash long enough for him to glance away from the huge globe through which they had been viewing the phenomenon in the sky.

The instant was long enough for him to become aware of his surroundings ... and to understand that they would all die if they remained above-ground under the influence of whatever was hap-

pening in the west. He managed to take two steps
forward and stumbled down the first stair. The instant he moved away from the globe under the
canopy that covered the underground entrance, his
mind cleared, and he reached up and grabbed Dale
and Zarkov down toward him, the three of them
stumbling like zombies away from the fantastic
colors and sounds.

"Flash?" Dale whimpered, but she did not resist
his pull, nor did Zarkov, as Flash led them down to
the lit corridor that was at least fifteen meters
below the level of the mall.

They stood at the bottom of the stairs, and
Zarkov stared back up, a look of awe on his features.

"What was it?" Flash asked, and Zarkov turned
slowly to look at him.

"I don't know," he said shaking his head. He
seemed almost sad, and he looked back up the
stairs again. "I've never experienced anything like
that in my life."

Dale was completely shaken, her complexion a
pasty white, but she too followed Zarkov's gaze up
the stairs. It seemed as if the two of them wanted to
climb back up to the mall, the hold on them hyp-
notic.

The effect on Flash was fading enough so that he
became aware of where they had come. They stood
in a wide corridor of spotlessly white walls and a
high ceiling that ran in the same direction as the
mall. In the distance to the west, Flash could make
out what appeared to be a widening in the corridor.
They would have to take refuge down here at least
for the night, he figured. If they remained by the

stairs it was possible that either Dale or Zarkov would try to go back outside.

He bodily pulled Dale and Zarkov around the corner from the stairs, and a couple of meters down the corridor they both began to recover.

Zarkov shuddered and shook his head in bewilderment. "It was like a dream," he said softly, looking up into Flash's eyes. Then he turned to his niece. "Are you all right, Dale?"

Dale was shivering, but she managed to nod. "I think so," she said. "Was it real, uncle? I mean, did all those things really happen?"

"What things?" Flash asked, and Dale looked at him for a moment almost as if he was a stranger. But then recognition dawned in her eyes.

"You were there," she said. "At least I think you were."

"Where?" Flash persisted.

A dreamy, faraway expression crossed her features, but she shook herself out of it. "I don't know," she said. "It was so real, but now I can't remember . . . exactly."

A flash of multicolored light briefly illuminated the stairwell, then began to die, and the three of them instinctively shrank farther away. Another brilliant burst of light reflected off the corridor wall opposite the stairwell, and Flash felt himself being drawn forward, as the reflected patterns on the wall moved and danced.

"No," Dale shrieked, and Flash grabbed her and Zarkov by the arm, and together the three of them turned their backs on the stairwell and hurried as fast as they could down the corridor.

The musical tones, if they could be called that,

seemed to follow them down the wide corridor as
they ran, but mercifully their effect diminished
rapidly the farther they got from the opening to the
mall above. Finally they came to a huge room.

The corridor walls opened to the left into a
cavernous room that looked more like a trans-
Earth shuttle station than anything else. The corridor they had come down was only one of dozens
of openings from the huge room, some of the corridors containing single tracks, much like a
monorail system.

Overhead, suspended from the ceiling, was a
three-sided plate that looked very much like a visiscreen, now blank, that Flash immediately understood was there to indicate transport arrival and
departure information.

Again he had the strong feeling that he had been
here before; that this place had been built by hu-
mans; that its purpose was familiar. And yet it was
all strange.

Dale evidently felt the same things, because she
uttered a little gasp of delight and understanding.
"A subway station," she said, but then her voice
died as a shuttle car came out of one of the corridors, and glided smoothly and silently to a stop in
the middle of the room.

The car was long and narrow with low sides and
richly shaped contour seats that could accommodate at least a dozen human-sized beings.

"Do you get the feeling that this is all familiar?"
Flash said, staring at the shuttle car almost as if it
was some kind of an apparition.

Zarkov looked at him and nodded. "The city,
the highway, the animals, and now this . . . yes," he

said. "Everything except whatever it was in the sky."

"Most of the technology isn't anything beyond us," Flash said, still staring at the car.

"Basically no, it doesn't seem to be," Zarkov said, obviously choosing his words with care. "And yet it is. Everything seems simple. Almost too simple."

Flash turned and looked back down the corridor. Even from here he could see the fantastic display of lights undulating like something with its own life down from the stairwell. They could not go back there. Forward was the only direction open to them. It was almost as if they were being herded in this direction, but by whom and for what purpose, Flash could not even guess.

A chime sounded, and instinctively they all looked up in time to see streams of symbols and diagrams moving rapidly across the overhead visiscreen.

Another similar chime sounded on the shuttle car itself, and a moment later the vehicle moved away, and then disappeared down one of the corridors. The overhead screen went blank.

"The city functions," Zarkov said, half to himself.

Flash was about to reply when another of the shuttle cars suddenly appeared from one of the corridors, and glided silently to a stop in the center of the terminal.

"We can't stay here," Flash said. He started toward the car, but Zarkov stopped him.

"We don't know where it's going," the scientist said.

Flash turned back. "Nor will we be able to figure that out from here." He looked at Dale. "We can't stay here. We can't go back outside. At least not tonight."

Zarkov and Dale said nothing.

"If we're going to survive we're going to have to explore."

"But systematically," Zarkov said.

The overhead chime sounded again, and once more streams of incomprehensible information flashed across the overhead screen. A moment afterward, the chime on the shuttle car sounded and the machine moved out of the terminal.

"If this is some kind of a subway transportation system, which it probably is, there has to be a map around here. Some means of determining which car goes where."

Another car glided in from one of the corridors, stopping in the middle of the terminal, and this time the three of them went across the room to it. There were no symbols on the vehicle, nor were there any kind of controls. Just the car itself and the contour seats.

"Flash," Dale cried, and Flash and Zarkov snapped around in time to see several of the janitor robots coming their way from the corridor they had taken.

"On the shuttle, quick," Flash shouted. As they scrambled aboard, the overhead chime sounded, and the visiscreen came alive.

Within a moment or two the car would be moving away, but the janitor robots were closing fast.

"Come on . . . come on . . ." Flash shouted in frustration.

The chime on the car sounded as the first of the robots, its claws extended, was less than two meters away, and a moment later the vehicle began moving toward a corridor, slowly at first, but then rapidly picking up speed, and suddenly they were out of the terminal, and the car accelerated, pushing them back into their contour seats.

For better or worse, Flash had the fleeting thought, they were on their way. But to where he did not want to hazard a guess, as the corridor sloped sharply downward and the car picked up even more speed.

# CHAPTER 11

The shuttle car continued its rapid descent into the bowels of the planet with no illusion of speed other than the blurred corridor walls rushing past them. There was no sound, no wind, no lurching. And yet the car neither slowed nor deviated from its sharply downward path.

They had not eaten or drunk since early morning before they had entered the city. Zarkov was a pathetic figure hunched in his contour seat next to Flash, and for the last ten minutes of the long shuttle ride the old scientist had said nothing, his mind apparently directed inward to his own private thoughts.

Dale too was quiet as she stared forward at the featureless, unchanging corridor ahead of them, her hands gripping the seat rests so tightly her knuckles had turned white.

Step by inexorable step, beginning with the *Goodhope* in Earth orbit, they had been led to this point. Whether they had been directed by some intelligence monitoring their progress, or whether it had been nothing more than automatic responses of ancient machinery still functioning without any sentient direction, Flash could not be certain.

He did know, however, that unless there was food and drink at the end of this trip, Zarkov would probably not last the night, and certainly not through tomorrow.

By this point Flash was sure they had come at least a hundred kilometers, perhaps more, beneath the surface of the planet, and he turned to ask Zarkov what he thought, when they burst out of the corridor into a cavern the size of which boggled the imagination.

Dale gasped, and Zarkov looked up out of his lethargy as the shuttle car shot out across an apparently bottomless pit along a slender rail that seemed to have no support. Huge arches of some glowing crystalline substance spanned the cavern, the ends lost in the distance. Machinery of every shape and description filled the open space like trees in a forest, with no apparent top and no apparent base.

Banks of lights flashed, great masses of shifting colors haloed incomprehensible objects, the size of which alone was enough to border on the unbelievable.

And yet, despite the mammoth size of what they were seeing, the machinery all seemed to be vaguely familiar, like everything else they had seen on this planet. But instead of lending comfort, the feeling was unsettling.

The opposite wall came rushing up at them from

the distance, and the shuttle car flashed into a corridor opening, and once again the walls rushing
past them were the only things they could see.

"What was it?" Dale asked.

Zarkov was slowly shaking his head. "I don't
know," he said, his voice ragged.

Flash leaned over a little closer to the old man.
"Are you all right, doc?"

Zarkov looked at him, his eyes watering slightly.
"I don't know, Flash. I'm tired."

A thin bead of perspiration had formed on
Zarkov's upper lip, and his color had paled, lending a waxy, unhealthy pallor to his skin. Flash was
suddenly very frightened for his old friend.

Again without warning the shuttle car burst out
into a mammoth cavern filled with equipment,
spanned as far as they could see, only by the
single, thin monorail that led straight through the
maze of gigantic machinery.

After a long time the rail began to angle even
more sharply downward, and with the change in
direction the car seemed to go even faster, the huge
columns of machinery rising higher and higher
above them, still with no bottom in sight—just
lights and equipment as far as they could see in any
direction.

"Uncle!" Dale suddenly shouted, and she
reached out to grab Zarkov's arm.

Flash, who had been staring at the fantastic
sights around him, snapped around in time to see
Zarkov clutching at his chest. The old man's face
had turned gray, and sweat poured from his brow,
his mouth screwed up in an expression of intense
agony.

Flash shifted in his seat as best he could, and loosened the collar of Zarkov's jump suit. The old man's breath came in ragged gasps, but there was nothing they could do about it.

"Hans," Flash shouted, but it did not seem as if Zarkov was hearing him. "Hans, you've got to fight it!" Zarkov's eyes seemed to focus and unfocus as he turned and stared into Flash's eyes. Tears were streaming down Dale's cheeks and she seemed to want to touch her uncle, but she did not know what to do to help him. She was shaking uncontrollably.

But then the spasm seemed to pass, and the look of intense pain eased slowly from Zarkov's features. After a time he began to breathe more easily, and his color began returning by slow degrees.

The old man tried to speak and could not. He moved to sit forward, but Flash held him back.

"Take it easy, doc," Flash said. "Sit back now and relax."

"It's his heart," Dale said through her tears. "He refuses to see a doctor. He needs tissue regeneration. But he said he'd attend to it later. He said he didn't have the time." There was a bitter note in her voice.

Below them, what appeared to be a city rose up from the distance, and still the shuttle car continued its downward plunge on the single, thin rail. Huge multicolored spires and wide, flat cubes shimmered in the artificial light that seemed to have no source, but shone everywhere.

The closer the shuttle car came to the lowest levels of this cavern, however, the more clear it became that they were approaching not a city, but nothing more than the base of the awesome machinery that rose up seemingly without end above them.

And then, describing a sweeping hyperbolic curve, the monorail swooped under a huge arch, slowed its high rate of speed smoothly, and finally came to a halt at the center of a park-like area at least a kilometer or more on a side. Well-tended green grass, fruit trees, and shrubbery of all sizes and shapes grew in perfect patterns, interspersed here and there with fountains like the ones in the mall above, spewing fantastically shaped sprays of water into bubbling pools.

From all directions monorail tracks led down from the ceiling that covered the park a couple of hundred meters overhead. Nowhere were there supports of any kind for the roof far above—it was just there, in all directions, beyond which the vague shapes of the towering machinery and the citylike structures seemed like a fantastic forest off in the distance, connected to this place by hundreds of monorails that disappeared into thin threads as far as the eye could see.

Flash and Dale helped the ailing Zarkov from the shuttle car, and a moment after they had lain him on the grass, the car moved away, and in a tremendous burst of speed, climbed up the hyperbolic curve of the rail, and was lost in the distance.

When Zarkov seemed to have caught his breath, Dale and Flash helped him across the wide lawn to the nearest fountain, where they helped him drink some water before they themselves drank.

Dale hurriedly gathered several varieties of fruit from a number of trees growing nearby, and, heedless of the risk they were taking, the three of them sat, their backs against the low structure of the fountain, eating as they watched the shuttle cars coming down the widely curved tracks from above. Each of them stopped for a few moments at the center of the park, and then departed as silently as they had come.

"All roads lead to Rome," Zarkov said softly after they had rested for at least a half hour.

"What?" Flash asked.

Zarkov shook his head and managed a slight smile. "Nothing," he said. "It was an ancient Earth expression."

"At least we know we can take one of the shuttles back to the surface any time we want," Dale said.

It was apparent to Flash that she was looking for some assurance, any assurance, that everything was going to work out. But Zarkov had been correct when he had warned them that they might not find anything helpful in the city. Despite the feeling of familiarity Flash had about this place, there had been little of anything that he had seen which could even have been potentially helpful to them. And considering not only the size of the vast underground caverns filled with machinery, but the size and the danger of the city above them, the task of finding anything useful seemed hopeless.

He felt at this moment like the savage suddenly transported into a deserted New Los Angeles that Zarkov had hypothesized. This place was fascinating and yet incomprehensible. Worse, it held dangers that none of them could even imagine.

Flash got to his feet after a long while. They were

going to have to try to find some repository of
knowledge, such as a library or a data center.
Someplace where they could learn the history of
this place—who built it, why they left; and then
perhaps a blueprint or a planetary map. Somewhere on this planet, or beneath it, there had to be
something to help them survive.

"Where are you going?" Zarkov asked, looking
up. His color was much better and the last vestiges
of pain had left his expression.

"You and Dale stay here. I'm going to have a
look around."

"No," Zarkov said sharply, and he tried to
struggle to his feet.

Dale jumped up and helped her uncle to stand.

"We've got to stick together," Zarkov said.
You've already seen what can happen. We have no
way of telling what might happen next. Together
we have a chance. Separated we wouldn't."

"Are you up to it, doc?" Flash asked.

Zarkov shrugged. "It's a moot point, Flash. We
can't just sit here by the fountain."

"Nor can we go back up, at least until morning,"
Dale said with a shudder.

They moved slowly away from the fountain to
one of the walkways that crisscrossed the park, and
headed toward the center of the huge area.

In the distance they could see a low, gray structure that appeared to be some kind of a building,
and they headed toward it, realizing almost immediately that all the walkways in the park led toward the central structure. They also could see that
all of the shuttles were stopping by one of the walkways leading to the building.

"The entire purpose of the shuttle system, it would appear, is to provide access to this place," Zarkov said as they walked.

"It must have been important," Flash said.

As they got closer they could see that the building was shaped in an octagon with dark openings on each of the eight sides. Between the doorways the material of the building, which looked like the same stone the city above them had been constructed from, was carved in delicate patterns that from a distance looked like a filigree.

Ringing the building was a wide walkway made of a soft plastic, all the walkways throughout the park ending up here. From where they stood opposite one of the eight entrances to the building, they could see that the delicate etchings between the portals were not merely a filigree decoration, they seemed to be writing of some kind.

"Instructions?" Dale asked, turning to her uncle.

Zarkov had been lost deep in thought, and when Dale spoke to him it took a moment for him to look up. When he did, he nodded. "That is probably a very close guess, my dear. I'm sure that's what those markings are." He turned to his young friend. "I think we've found your library, Flash."

"This was a central information bank?"

"I think so," Zarkov said, and he moved forward across the circular walkway toward one of the doorways. He stopped less than a meter away and tried to look inside, but it was totally dark. He moved a couple of steps closer, and reached out with his hand.

"Be careful, uncle," Dale said, moving toward him, but Zarkov's hand disappeared inside the doorway, and a moment later he pulled it back, a startled expression on his face.

"What is it?" Flash asked, moving quickly to the scientist's side.

"A matter transmitter," Zarkov said slowly, and he looked again at the portal. "We're just coming up with the basic theory, but our technology is nowhere near this point."

He moved a little closer to the portal, almost as if he was being drawn forward, but Flash pulled him gently back. "Hang on now, doc. We have no idea where this leads, or what its purpose was. It could have been connected with some kind of religion. This could be the place where people who wanted to die came. Maybe it leads nowhere. Or maybe whatever it's for, or wherever it leads, is a one-way ticket. Maybe it even leads off the planet."

"I don't think so, Flash," Zarkov said carefully. "There was too much traffic here. Too many shuttles coming and going for it to be some kind of religious suicide instrument."

"Then where are all the people?" Dale asked softly. "Maybe they *did* all come down here and do away with themselves."

"I don't think so," Zarkov said, and he turned again to face the portal, and before Flash or Dale could stop him, he quickly stepped forward and was gone.

"Uncle!" Dale shrieked, and she tried to follow him but Flash held her back.

"Wait," he shouted, and he pulled her a few steps farther away from the opening as the darkness began to shimmer, and then Zarkov stepped back out onto the walkway.

Dale rushed to him and threw her arms around his neck. "My God, uncle, you frightened me."

Zarkov patted her shoulder. "Everything is all right, my dear. Nothing to be frightened of."

When Dale was sufficiently calmed down, she parted from her uncle and looked at him with reproach. "That was a silly thing for you to do."

"On the contrary," he said, "someone had to do it, and I was the logical choice." He turned to Flash. "It would appear this is indeed the central computer bank. I'd guess that the shuttle craft brought the inhabitants down here from the city on a regular basis for information and probably serious research."

"Is it a matter transmitter?"

"I think so. The room I was just in is huge, almost as large as this entire park. Obviously used for research, probably in astronomy or astrophysics."

"Do you think you can activate the system?" Flash asked.

Zarkov shrugged. "I don't know. But I think I'd like to try."

"Will we be able to find a way home?" Dale asked excitedly.

"Not so fast," Zarkov said. "We may find nothing that we can understand. And there may be a certain amount of risk involved."

"What do you mean?" Dale asked.

"I don't know for sure," the old man said thoughtfully. "But so far everything we've seen on this planet has had an attendant risk."

"Everything except this park," Dale said, looking over her shoulder.

"We may not have been here long enough to activate whatever protective systems there might be."

"Now you've got me frightened again," Dale said.

"I don't want you frightened, my dear. I just want you to be careful."

"Let's go then," Flash said after a moment.

Zarkov hesitated an instant longer, and then turned and once again disappeared through the portal. Dale followed immediately on his heels, and a second later Flash stepped into the dark opening.

A tingling sensation rose through his entire body, and for an instant he was in an area of total darkness. Then he stepped into a huge room and found Zarkov and Dale waiting for him a few steps away.

What were obviously visiscreens lined all four walls. Suspended from the ceiling were several devices that looked very much like astrogation tank models. And hundreds of tables, each with its own contour chair, visiscreen, and some kind of a control panel, were arranged in rows throughout the large room. Each of the tables was set up in such a position that the user could have an unobstructed view of the overhead equipment as well as the large visiscreens on at least one wall.

There was only one entrance to the room, however, and it was the one they had come through.

"Wait here a moment," Flash said, suddenly getting a glimmering of an idea, and before Zarkov or Dale could object, he stepped back through the portal and once again outside into the park. He hurried around the building to one of the other entrances, and stepped through it.

This time he found himself in a room, the same size as the first one, but filled with dozens of jungle and mountain scenes complete with moving animals, a breeze, and moving water.

He remained staring at the things in the room for only a moment, before he stepped back through the doorway, went around the building to the third entrance, and stepped through it.

This room was filled with a huge diagram that curved around all four walls, and even as Flash watched, various lines and indicator lights on the diagram shifted and changed colors and intensities. The center of the room was dominated by a huge circular control console, across which patterns of lights shifted and changed. The room was probably used to monitor and study planetary power systems.

Flash had taken a few steps into the room and when he turned to go back through the doorway into the park, he came face to face with a black, humanlike machine that stood at least a half a head taller than him.

For a long moment Flash did not move as he studied the thing that had evidently just come through the portal. It had a symmetrical, delicate-looking body; two legs, each with three joints, were attached to a featureless torso, as were two arms that ended in hands, each with a dozen multi-jointed digits. The head was wedge-shaped and contained two lighted sensory devices that looked like the many faceted eyes of an Earth insect of some kind.

The entire effect seemed malevolent, and Flash felt a sudden surge of fear for Dale and Zarkov.

The android said something in a language that almost sounded like old Earth English, its voice flat and emotionless with a slight echo.

When Flash did not respond, the machine's head turned slightly to the left, almost as if it were looking over its shoulder, or listening for something in the distance, and then it turned back, and spoke again.

"I don't understand . . ." Flash started to say, when he heard Dale's scream and Zarkov shouting, but somehow the sounds were coming from the android. He leapt forward, knocking the machine back through the portal, and before the device could respond, he was back out in the park, racing toward the room where he had left his friends.

# CHAPTER 12

Every place they had been on this planet had had its own attendant protective devices. The jungle had had its bear creatures. The city above, its janitor robots. And now here, the black machines. But none of the protective devices was beyond defeat, and none of them seemed to match the wondrous technology obvious in the city above, nor the fabulous machinery in the vast subterranean caverns. It was as if the robots had been added as an afterthought by someone or something other than the original builders of this place.

The walkway outside the octagon was deserted as Flash raced to the portal through which he had left Zarkov and Dale. He was certain he had heard Dale's scream coming from some kind of an audio pickup on the machine that had confronted him. But what it meant he could not guess.

Without hesitation he leapt through the

doorway into the astrophysics room, and in the instant it took for him to regain his orientation he saw Dale and Zarkov being bodily carried toward the back of the huge room between the rows of tables by two machines that were exactly like the one he had run into.

Something hard slammed into Flash's shoulder as he was about to move away from the doorway, sending him sprawling to his knees, the wind knocked out of him.

He managed to roll over in time to see one of the machines coming toward him, and he kicked out with his right foot in a classic Tri-V maneuver, catching the robot at one of the joints in its left leg.

The material the machine was constructed from was brittle, and its leg snapped, sending it clattering to the floor in a heap, its arms waving dangerously close to Flash, who jumped up and away from its grasp.

It was a machine, but it was not invincibly beyond human strength. And that thought gave Flash some hope as he swiveled, still trying to catch his breath, and raced down the long rows of tables toward the retreating figures of Dale, Zarkov, and their captors.

Flash caught up to Dale and Zarkov on the far side of the room as a wide door slid open beneath one of the large visiscreens.

Zarkov was unconscious, but Dale was struggling wildly against the machine that was bodily carrying her, and when she saw Flash closing in on them, she screamed again, and fought all the harder.

Dale's machine, oblivious to her struggles, carried her through the doorway, but Zarkov's machine turned, released the scientist, who slumped to the floor, and stepped away to meet Flash's running charge.

Flash barreled into the robot, lowering his head and ramming its torso with his powerful shoulder. As the door through which Dale had been taken closed, the machine Flash had slammed into went down, hitting one of the tables, cracking the back of its torso amid a shower of sparks.

The robot twitched wildly, flipping over the table, smashing the small visiscreen, and breaking some of the indicators on the control panel, but then it righted itself, and advanced on Flash, its arms swinging crazily.

Flash grabbed Zarkov and pulled him away from the machine, which suddenly began whirling in circles, almost as if it were blind, swinging its arms powerfully in all directions.

Zarkov's eyes fluttered open, and he grabbed Flash's arm in a convulsive grip. "Dale," he gasped. "It's got Dale!"

The machine, evidently responding to Zarkov's voice, snapped around and came their way, its movements spasmodic, almost as if it were barely able to operate for lack of lubricant.

Flash dragged Zarkov farther behind one of the tables, and then shoved one of the heavy contour chairs out in the machine's path.

The robot seemed to hesitate a moment, but then it stumbled into the chair, tried to climb over it, but failed, falling sideways and snapping its left arm off at the torso. A shower of sparks sprayed like a Roman candle from the machine's arm socket, and then sputtered and suddenly stopped as the machine finally ceased functioning.

Flash's heart was hammering and he took a deep breath to calm himself before he went back to Zarkov, who had managed to sit up and was trying to pull himself to his feet using the edge of the table as a support.

He helped the old man up and immediately Zarkov searched the room with his eyes, holding on to Flash's arm for support.

"Where is she?" Zarkov said, his voice ragged and weak, but with much fear.

"The robot took her," Flash said.

Zarkov looked up into his eyes, anguish on his face. "They were waiting for us. I knew something like this was going to happen. Oh, God . . . Flash . . ."

"Take it easy, doc, we'll find her," Flash said. He was very worried about his old friend. The lack of proper rest and food over the past day and a half was making its mark not only on the aging scientist's body, but on his mind as well. Flash did not think Zarkov could take much more of this. But in the back of his own mind was despair as well. Considering the complexity of this planet, he seriously doubted if they'd ever find Dale, no matter what they did.

He propped Zarkov up against the table and went past the downed robot to the wall beneath the visiscreen where the doorway had been. There was no sign, however, that there had ever been an opening here. There were no hinges, no slides, not even a hairline crack to show where the door would have been in the soft patina of the rocklike material of the wall.

Zarkov had been watching his every move, and when Flash turned back finally, defeat on his face, Zarkov paled even more than he had before, all the blood seemingly leaving his face.

"She's gone," the old man said, burying his face in his hands. "She's gone and I could have prevented it."

Flash took his old friend's shoulder. "There was nothing you could have done. I should never have left you two alone. You warned me. We should have stuck together."

Zarkov looked up, grief in his eyes. "I could have fought back. I could have done something."

Flash was shaking his head. "No, Hans," he said gently. "I very nearly didn't make it myself, and I'm younger and stronger than you."

Zarkov said nothing, but he was filled with emotion.

"We'll find her," Flash said. "Between us we'll find her. All we have to do is figure out where they took her."

A spark of interest suddenly rose in Zarkov's eyes, the scientist in him beginning to overcome the old, devoted uncle. "No," he said slowly, as if he were thinking out loud. "Not where she was taken, but why they took her. That's the key. *Why.*"

"We are the intruders," Flash said. "You said it yourself. We've been running into protective systems."

Zarkov shook his head. "If that was the case this time, there would have been more robots. They would have sent more and more of them to capture us as well."

Flash was beginning to understand what Zarkov was trying to tell him. But it didn't make any sense.

"She's a hostage?" he asked.

"It would appear so," Zarkov said, and he turned away from Flash to gaze around the large room and at its equipment.

"Then this planet is inhabited after all."

Zarkov looked back. "Not necessarily. From what we've seen so far, the beings who built this place were highly sophisticated. Far more so than the Federation."

"Agreed," Flash said.

"Which means the robots, as crude as they are, could be directed by a highly sophisticated computer system that understands sentient being values. You're the xenosociologist, Flash—what do you think? Could a computer system understand the concept of hostage liability?"

"If we presupposed love or some form of affection as a legitimate value . . . a legitimate universal value . . . yes, it's possible. Sentient beings tend to build into their more sophisticated machines at least some of their own values. Look at our own cybernetic control limitations."

Again Zarkov looked toward the wall through which Dale had been taken. "Then it is possible she is a hostage."

"If that's the case, it means we have to sit and wait for whatever demands are made on us. Providing we can communicate."

Zarkov turned once again to Flash. There was an intense look in her eyes. "Where did you go when you left us?"

"I had an idea about the other seven portals. I didn't see any other entrances to this room," Flash said. He felt a stab of guilt about it. Had he not left them, there was a very good chance Dale would not have been taken.

"I thought so," Zarkov said, the excitement mounting in him. "What did you find?"

"I got into only two of the rooms before I was confronted by one of the robots. One of the rooms looked like a world model of some sort. There were scenes of mountains, jungles, and oceans, complete with wild life and vegetation."

"And the other room?"

"It looked like a power control center, or at least a study center for planetary power consumption systems."

Zarkov seemed to draw inward for several long moments, but then he looked up, genuine excitement in his eyes. "That's it, then," he said, pushing away from the table. His legs wobbled and Flash grabbed his left arm to steady him.

"What's it?" Flash asked.

"If Dale is indeed a hostage, and if indeed a demand will be made on us, probably for our surrender, and probably to a machine, we have to counter their offer."

"What do you mean?"

"On the way down here, through the caverns, and now this place . . . what did all of it tell you?"

"I don't know," Flash started to say, but then he checked himself. "It looked familiar. But I just don't know."

"I do," Zarkov said. "This place convinced me. We're in a world data center, if you want to call it that. Here in this building are apparently eight separate rooms or learning centers—perhaps even control or modification centers—from which all the knowledge of this world could be taped."

"All right," Flash said slowly. "It seems like a reasonable assumption from what we've seen."

"Such a system would need support. I mean it would need machinery to make it all work. Data storage. Recall. Control. Power."

Flash could see what Zarkov was getting at. "What we went through coming down here . . . the vast caverns . . . it was all a gigantic computer."

"Why not?" Zarkov asked. "Certainly some of the machinery we saw was power equipment. Perhaps much of it to run the city, and perhaps other cities around this planet. But a part of it must have provided the power and control for this building."

"So we pull the plug," Flash started to say, but Zarkov cut him off impatiently.

"There would be no such thing as a 'plug,' " he said. "But you tell me—what's the most important section of any computer, bio or nonbio?"

"Memory," Flash said automatically.

"Indeed," Zarkov said. "The computer's memory. Its data storage center. Its heart. If we threaten to destroy it, the machine, if it is at all sophisticated —and I believe it will be by its actions and by what we've seen of the city above—it will value its memory above all else."

"And it will protect its memory above all else," Flash said, an ominous feeling growing inside of him.

"Yes," Zarkov answered softly. "It might even try to hide its memory from discovery, but it will not be able to."

For a moment Flash was confused again, but then he understood finally and completely what

Zarkov had been trying to say to him all along. Without a word he helped the old man down the long row of tables to the portal in front of which the machine that he had put out of commission still lay twitching.

They sidestepped the robot and stepped through the portal into the park. Still there were no more of the machines visible, but Flash suspected it would not be long before the central computer figured out what it was they were up to, and would be sending out other machines to stop them. They would have to hurry not only on that account, but also because of Dale. There was no telling what was happening to her at this moment, or what would happen to her unless they were successful, and quickly so.

They hurried around the building to the power room that Flash had been in earlier, and stepped through the portal. For several long seconds they stood just within the doorway as Zarkov studied the huge display board that swept grandly around the huge room, trying to make some sense from the complex diagrams and shifting patterns of lights.

"That's it," Zarkov finally said, half to himself, and Flash helped him across the room to the massive circular control console.

Patterns of lights similar to the indicators on the main display board shifted across the console, below which were row after row of small multi-colored plates, each with its own symbol in a writing that looked similar in style to the delicate filagree etchings on the outside of the building.

Without any further hesitation, Zarkov reached out and delicately touched one of the tiny plates. Instantly there was a slight shift in one section of the lights on the console. A corresponding change in pattern appeared in more detail on the main display board on the walls.

Zarkov touched the same plate once more, and another shift in the pattern of lights occurred.

"We'll never figure this out," Flash said.

"We don't have to," Zarkov said. He pointed across the room to a section of the display board that showed a steady pattern of lights. Directly above it was another series of lights that continued to shift along a circular pattern. "I'd guess that section indicates the power drain for the city above us, and the circular section is whatever is happening in the sky."

Zarkov searched the control console for the matching section, and when he found it he began touching buttons and the lights indicating the city's functions, began winking out a row at a time.

"We can turn off the city," Flash said somewhat impatiently. "So what?"

Zarkov, whose fingers were playing over the control console, glanced up. "We can turn off the entire planet and all of its functions from here. Or at least we can start to do that."

Other lights on the display board were going out now, while along some sections the patterns began shifting faster and faster.

"There's going to come a point where the central computer is going to conclude that someone is working the control console to the detriment of planetary systems. When that happens, unless I miss my bet, it'll begin to interfere."

Zarkov was working his way down the control console, hitting hundreds of the tiny plates, his fingers dancing faster and faster. The display board had gone wild; huge sections of lights were flickering out, while other sections began glowing an angry red as increasingly complex patterns raced across banks of indicators.

And then the walls began to shimmer and blur.

Flash was the first to notice that something was happening. As the lights in the huge room began to dim, he looked up. His immediate impression was that his eyes were going bad, but then as he stared at the display board close by, and it too began to fade.

"Doc?" Flash said, grabbing Zarkov's arm.

The old man looked up, and then stopped what he was doing. "It's happening," he said.

The walls and above them the ceiling were fading fast, becoming transluscent, and beyond the display board they could see what appeared to be the interior of a vast honeycomb.

As the control console itself shimmered and faded in front of them, Zarkov studied the last section of control plates he had touched, but then the console was gone and both men looked up.

The room they had been in had completely disappeared. Now they were in the center of a huge, golden-colored honeycomb that seemed to be alive with a low-pitched, dull hum. It was warmer here, and the floor beneath their feet seemed soft, almost as if they were standing on the broad belly of some huge, living creature.

The individual sections of the maze went straight up as far as they could see, and narrow walkways seemed to radiate in every direction like the spokes of some gigantic wheel. Each compartment of the honeycomb was about one meter in diameter, and seemed illuminated with a soft, golden light from somewhere deep inside the maze.

Neither of them had moved from their spot, but now Zarkov stumbled forward, and with Flash's help they slowly moved away from the hub areas and down one of the narrow paths through the honeycomb. The narrow opening went straight as far as they could see, as did the other paths.

"Repititive patterns," Zarkov said. "The computer's memory. It has to be."

"What about the building and the park?" Flash asked. He spoke in a hushed voice. This place was almost like a church, or a library.

Zarkov looked up at Flash and smiled. "It was a matter transmitter all right. But instead of transmitting us to some spot on the planet, it transmitted each individual room as well as the park to this spot. We were standing in the heart of the machine's memory all along. The building and park were transmitted here. Which is a nifty bit of physics."

"Two objects occupying the same space at the same time," Flash said, raising his eyebrows.

"Perhaps the same space, but not the same time," Zarkov said, chewing at his lower lip. "It could be done, I suppose, by modulating or multiplexing real time and space. For a brief instant the room existed in a given place. The next instant the memory banks were there and the room was someplace else. The following instant the room was back, and so on."

"What about Dale?" Flash asked.

A grim expression crossed Zarkov's features,

and he stopped walking and turned around. "Let's go back."

"And do what?"

Zarkov looked up. "It's possible that the hub area is the central axis of the computer's memory banks. We're going to go back and began destroying the honeycomb at the hub, if we can, a section at a time."

The enormity of what Zarkov was saying took several long seconds to have any effect on Flash. But when it did, it stopped him in his tracks.

"You can't be serious, doc."

"Very," Zarkov said. "The computer knew we were here. It knew that we crash-landed. It knew that we came into the city, and it tried to have us destroyed. It also knew that we were coming close to its memory, and it tried to stop us again, carrying Dale off when we fought back."

"So now you're going to take revenge?"

Zarkov laughed and patted Flash on the arm. "Not revenge," he said as they came back to the hub. "I want its attention and cooperation."

# CHAPTER 13

In all the years Flash had known Dr. Zarkov, he
had come to love and respect the old man for a
number of reasons, among them his gentleness and
understanding. He could never remember seeing
Zarkov unreasonable, but at this moment, standing in the midst of a vast, fabulous machine, he was
seeing a side of his old friend that he had never
even suspected existed.

"Are you sure you want to do this, doc?" Flash
asked one last time.

Zarkov, who had advanced to the edge of one of
the columns of honeycombs, glanced back at
Flash, looked away, and then did a double take,
evidently catching the deep concern in Flash's eyes.
"They've taken Dale," he replied.

"Yes," Flash said, and the thought that Dale
was at this moment with the robots caused a deep
ache inside of him. Yet what they were about to do
was wrong; he felt that deeply as well. "If they had
wanted to harm her, they would not have bothered

174

to carry her off. You said so yourself. She's a hostage."

"We're going to change that situation," Zarkov said, his voice still low, but even.

"Then let's try to communicate with the machine, not destroy it."

"Our personal well-being aside, Flash," Zarkov said, "what about the men and women aboard the *Goodhope?*" There was a menace in his voice. "It's very possible that this machine murdered them."

"What about the missing woman . . . Sandra Debonshire? Don't you believe she killed her shipmates and then jumped ship?"

"Except for the device in the drive room, I would have thought so. But this machine placed that unit aboard the Goodhope, and once someone was on board it directed the ship back here to a crash landing."

Flash shook his head and ran his fingers through his hair. "There's something wrong with the logic of that," he said.

"Yes," Zarkov replied softly. "But the faulty logic does not lie with us." He turned to look up at the honeycomb. "It lies here."

Once again Zarkov stepped forward, and gingerly reached out to touch the edge of one of the memory compartments, and the material it was made of crumbled with the lightest touch, a section about the size of the scientist's hand falling to the walkway.

Every muscle and nerve in Flash's body was taut. The machine would have to protect itself. He was certain that it would not allow what Zarkov was doing to continue.

The old man raised his arm as if to take a hefty swing at the delicate material when a burst of light shimmered at the edge of one of the pathways a few meters from where they stood.

Zarkov's hand stopped in mid-swing, and he and Flash both turned to look at the light, which seemed to drift in and out of focus. Finally it solidified to reveal Dale Arden standing there, holding her hands out in front of her as if she were a suppliant at an altar.

"Don't do that, Uncle Hans," she pleaded. Her voice sounded far away.

"Dale," Zarkov cried, and he took a step toward her.

"I'm not where I appear to be, uncle," she said. Her voice was strained, and on the verge of cracking. "This is just a holographic projection."

Flash stepped past Zarkov and looked closely at the image, and then he could see it was nothing more than a holograph, but a very good one. "Where are you?" he asked.

"Above you, in the city."

"Are you all right?" Zarkov asked. "Have they harmed you?"

"I'm fine, uncle. But you mustn't destroy the machine's memory. I'm told it can never be repaired."

"I will destroy it all unless you are immediately released unharmed."

Dale looked at something over her shoulder, and then turned back. "No," she said. "I heard what you and Flash were saying. We rushed as fast as we could to build a projector so that I could talk to you. Everything is not what it seems to be. You've got to believe me."

"Who's there with you?" Flash asked.

There was a haunted, strange look in her eyes, as she once again turned to look at something over her shoulder. "Everything will be explained to you. But you have to see it for yourself. You'd never believe it if I told you now."

"Can you come here?" Zarkov asked.

She shook her head. "No. No one can get down there for the moment. I don't know why yet, but you must come up here."

"They've done something to her," Zarkov said to Flash. "If we leave here we'll lose the advantage."

"Uncle," Dale cried. "Please, you must get out of there now. Just your presence in the memory banks is causing irreparable harm. Please!"

"Do you believe that you won't be harmed if we leave here?" Flash asked.

"Yes . . . yes," she cried. She seemed on the verge of collapse. "And so will you as soon as you come up."

Flash looked at Zarkov and the old scientist sighed deeply, and finally nodded his head.

"How do we get out of here?" Flash asked, and the relief on Dale's face was instantaneous.

"Step back into the hub and you'll be materialized into the power control room. From there take any shuttle to the surface. I'll be waiting for you."

"How will you know which shuttle station we'll be arriving at? There must be hundreds throughout the city."

"I'm told we can redirect whatever shuttle you take to the proper station."

"Are you sure you're all right, Dale?" Flash asked.

"Yes," she said. "I'm tired, and overawed, as you will be when you get here, but I'm all right. Now please hurry. I'm told that your body heat and moisture is destroying millions of cells."

Flash took Zarkov's arm and together they stepped back into the direct center of the hub. "We're ready," Flash said.

Dale's image disappeared, and the vast cavern filled with the machine's memory cells shimmered and wavered. The power control room they had been in before began to solidify around them.

The display board around the walls and the control console had been restored to their original status, and when the materialization was completed, Flash helped Zarkov away from the console to the portal.

Outside in the park they hesitated a moment on the circular walkway. "I wouldn't have destroyed the machine's memory, Flash." Zarkov said. His voice was sad. "I wanted the machine's attention, and I got it."

"I'm sorry I doubted you," Flash said contritely.

"You're a good man. Don't ever change," Zarkov said, and without another word they moved down one of the walkways and climbed aboard a shuttle that had just arrived.

A few moments later the transport moved away from the path and accelerated up the long, curved track from beneath the roof that covered the park, and headed toward the surface of the planet.

Zarkov laid his head back and closed his eyes, and during the long trip up, which took about twenty minutes, Flash was left to his own thoughts.

Foremost in his mind was Dale's well-being. She

had seemed strained, and near collapse, and yet there had been an underlying aura of satisfaction in her demeanor. It was as if she were an explorer who had come to the end of a long and arduous journey; she was worn out, but happy that the trip was over.

And, like Zarkov, Flash was worried that they had left behind their only advantage when they agreed to get out of the machine's memory units. If Dale had been coerced or drugged into saying the things that she had, all would be lost.

However, he thought to himself, they had had no other choice, and he too sat back in his seat and closed his eyes. For better or worse, their survival still depended upon what they found on this planet.

Dale was waiting for them in the shuttle station, as she had promised she would be, and when they arrived she rushed over to help her uncle out of the car with a little cry of joy and relief.

"Oh, God ... I was worried about you, Uncle Hans. I didn't know what to do when the city's power began going off and they told me that you and Flash were causing it."

Flash had climbed out of the car and stood behind Zarkov. "Who are *they?*" he asked.

She looked up at him. "You're in for a shock. Both of you are."

"Are you all right?" Flash asked.

She nodded. "Tired, as I said before. But I'm all right." She seemed to turn inward for a moment, but then she looked up again. "A lot of things are going to change for us in a little while, but my feelings for you won't."

Once again Flash got the distinct impression that she was satisfied, contented, and yet she seemed on the verge of falling over.

"It isn't far," she said finally, taking her uncle's arm. "And there is food and drink."

She led them down the long corridor, back to the stairs that led up to the level of the mall, and without hesitation they started up.

"What was that thing in the sky?" Flash asked as they took the stairs slowly for Zarkov's sake.

"I don't know yet," Dale said. "But it's gone now."

"And the janitor robots?" Zarkov asked.

Dale laughed. "That's exactly what they were. But they won't bother us either."

It was late at night, the air was cool and the sky dark, but the city was ablaze with lights although it still seemed deserted. At the head of the stairs they paused long enough for Zarkov to catch his breath, and then Dale led them along one of the paths past a beautiful fountain and across the mall to the base of one of the tremendous spires.

As they approached the building, which rose at least a thousand meters above the level of the mall, a section of the wall shimmered and dissolved, revealing a wide doorway. They passed through this and entered a huge lobby with a mosaic tile floor, vast expanses of what seemed to be glass windows that overlooked the mall, and a riot of trees and other growing things that rose at least a hundred meters to the ceiling.

Near the center of the vast lobby Dale took them into a cubicle that looked very much like an ordinary grav tube, but instead of the lurch of stepping into a field, there was nothing more than a slight tingling sensation, and almost instantly the lobby was gone, replaced with a wide corridor.

They stepped out of the cubicle, and Dale smiled nervously. "We're here," she said.

"Did we go up or down?" Flash asked.

"Up," she said. "We're on the top floor. The view is wonderful. You can see the waterfall from here, and the river going into the jungle beyond."

Zarkov had turned to look at the cubicle they had just stepped out of. "A matter transmitter?"

"I think so," she said. "I think they used them for a lot of things."

"Used?" Flash said. "Past tense?"

Dale nodded. "I don't know the entire story—we'll get that soon. But I do know that the people who built this place are gone. They've been gone for a very long time."

The corridor turned a sharp corner fifty meters away from the cubicle, and Dale led them to within less than a meter of it where she stopped again and faced them.

"Prepare yourself for a shock, uncle," she said softly. "I don't know all the details, but I know enough now to understand that something terribly important is happening here."

"I'm ready," Zarkov said, and Dale looked to Flash, who nodded.

The three of them stepped around the corner into a large, dimly lit room with floor to ceiling windows that afforded a magnificent view of the city far below them. The floor was carpeted with a material that seemed to be some kind of fur, and the room was furnished with low couches, chairs, and wide cocktail tables. At least a hundred and fifty people stood or sat talking in small groups, and when Dale, Zarkov, and Flash entered the room everyone looked their way.

A young man and woman, and an older, distinguished-looking man—all of them wearing spotlessly white coveralls—broke away from the group they were in by the window and hurried across the room.

Both Flash and Zarkov were speechless, and Dale seemed somewhat nervous and ill at ease.

"What have you told your friends?" the younger man asked Dale as he looked at Flash. He was a small man, at least a half a head shorter than Flash, and much thinner. He spoke English with an odd accent.

"Nothing," Dale said in a subdued voice. "I wanted them to hear the entire story from you, as you promised."

"As it shall be," the man said, and he stuck out his hand to Flash, who took it. "I'm Peter Van d'Hoef. Welcome to Citadel I, Colonel Gordon."

A chill swept through Flash and out of the corner of his eye he could see Zarkov paling at the man's name, which both of them recognized. "You were the captain of the *Goodhope?*"

Van d'Hoef smiled and nodded. He seemed like a pleasant man.

"You're dead," Flash blurted out, and the man laughed.

"Obviously not," he said, and he turned to Zarkov. "I'd like to welcome you especially, Dr. Zarkov. Your niece has told us much about you."

Zarkov inclined his head, but said nothing at first, his gaze directed to the young woman who returned his stare with an uncertain smile. "Sandra

Debonshire?" Zarkov asked finally, his voice barely audible.

The young woman nodded. "Yes," she said, and Zarkov turned to the older man, who smiled broadly and stuck out his hand.

"They call me Martin," he said, his voice smooth, well-modulated, but with the same accent as Van d'Hoef.

"Martin was the only resident of this planet before we arrived . . . or should I say, before he came out to get us . . . but he has never been a living creature in the strictest sense of the word. He is an android robot," Van d'Hoef said.

"Fascinating," Zarkov said half under his breath, and then he looked around the large room. "And the others? There are 158 of you?"

Van d'Hoef was nodding. "We're the crew and passengers of the Intersteller Exploration Ship *Goodhope,* outbound from Earth some two hundred years ago, Earth Time Reckoning."

Zarkov took a half step forward. "How long have you been here?"

"A hundred and twenty years."

"Eighty years out at sub-light speed you were awakened and taken off the *Goodhope?*" Zarkov asked.

Van d'Hoef nodded, but said nothing.

"You evidently returned to your ship at a faster-than-light speed to a spot earlier than your departure."

Van d'Hoef nodded again. "About fifteen years earlier."

Zarkov was shaking his head. "Then you should not be here now. Fifteen years after your death you

would have come back to the point where you left
your ship, and at that point would have ceased to
exist in the present tense."

A weariness seemed to come over the man. "We
try not to think about that." He glanced at the
young woman beside him, and they smiled at each
other. "We're not human either—not in the strictest sense of the word. But unlike Martin here, who
is constructed of nonbiological materials, we are
definitely biologic in makeup." He sighed deeply.
"In those first fifteen years, new bodies were constructed for us and our psyches were imprinted on
artificial brains. Not quite the same, but I don't
feel any different than before."

Zarkov's legs finally gave way, and Martin was
the first to react, grabbing the aging scientist before
he could actually fall to the floor.

"I think perhaps you should eat and rest before
we tell you the entire story," Van d'Hoef said.

Martin helped Zarkov across the room to the
couch, and Dale followed them, but Flash remained behind with Van d'Hoef.

"First, I want to know why you allowed us to
crash-land without sending someone out to try and
help us. We very nearly didn't make it," Flash said.
He was angry because he felt he had been manipu-
lated. And by a machine.

"We thought you were the enemy," Van d'Hoef
said simply.

"It was *your* ship," Flash snapped, his voice rising. "You, with the help of these machines, retro-
fitted the *Goodhope* with a faster-than-light drive
that brought us back here."

"No," Van d'Hoef said. "We did not."

# CHAPTER 14

It was morning, and Flash awoke with a start, guilty that he had not managed to remain awake through the night as he had wanted, to keep watch over Zarkov and Dale.

Despite his angry protests, Van d'Hoef and the crew of the *Goodhope* had refused to say anything further to them until they had rested.

"In the morning," Van d'Hoef had promised. "Then you'll be told everything."

They had been fed and put up in a pleasantly furnished bedroom on the same floor as the meeting hall, and Zarkov and Dale had both immediately flopped down on beds and fallen instantly asleep.

For a long time Flash had looked down at the city through a large window, but then he too had gone to his bed to lie back and relax, keeping his eye on the door across the room.

But he had been dead tired, the events of the past days too much even for his stamina, and he had finally drifted off.

He sat up now and looked across the room, and his heart nearly hammered out of his chest. Both of the other beds were empty. He was alone in the room.

He jumped out of bed just as the door opened and Dale came in. "Good morning," she said brightly, and she came across the room to him, stood up on tiptoes, and pecked him on the cheek. "Did you have a good sleep?"

"Where's your uncle?" Flash snapped.

"Everything is fine, Flash," she said placatingly. "He's with the others having breakfast. I was sent to wake you. They want to get started with our briefing."

Flash ran his fingers through his hair. "I wanted to stay awake last night. I didn't know what was going to happen. I don't trust them."

"They mean us no harm," she said. "But there is some sort of trouble."

"What do you mean?" Flash asked, looking sharply at her.

She shook her head. "I don't know for sure, but they all seemed worried, somehow. Even the android Martin seems concerned, but no one will say anything. Not until we're all together."

"Are they all in the meeting room?" Flash asked.

"No. It's only Van d'Hoef, Sandra, and Martin, besides us. The others had to return to work."

Flash had turned to look around the room, but then turned back. "Work?"

Dale nodded. "The *Goodhope*'s people built the janitor robots and the machines down in the data center that carried me off. That's why the technologies didn't match. They're all working on something else now. They wouldn't tell me what, but it's apparently important." She managed a slight smile, and nodded toward a door across the room. "There's a unit in there that's a lot like a pressure bath, only a lot nicer. When you're cleaned up, come on down to the meeting room. There'll be something for you to eat."

"I don't trust them, Dale. They let us struggle on our own in the jungle without so much as lifting a finger to help us. But once we were a threat to them, they suddenly became our gracious hosts."

"Uncle Hans said the same thing to Van d'Hoef, and he said it would all be explained this morning. He said we'd understand."

There was something wrong. Something drastically wrong . . . Flash could feel it thick in the air. And yet Dale seemed confident that although there might be some kind of trouble, they were safe here.

He sighed deeply and shrugged. "All right," he said. "I'll get cleaned up and meet you in a couple of minutes."

"Everything is going to work out, Flash," she said. "No matter what is happening here, these people are still from Earth. They're human beings."

"Granted," Flash said darkly. "But among them is a murderer."

"I know," Dale said weakly. "Van d'Hoef didn't say anything about it, except that a crew had gone out to look for the *Goodhope*'s wreckage."

"What did the android say?" Flash asked.

Dale shook her head. "I haven't spoken with him. He and Uncle Hans have been sitting together in a corner by the window talking since before I woke up."

* * *

Dale had been correct about the unit in the bathroom—it was a lot like a pressure bath, only it didn't use water. Yet when he stepped out of the machine and back into the bedroom, he felt clean and refreshed. A fresh set of white coveralls made of some kind of smooth, silky material, along with a pair of soft plastic boots, were laid out for him on the bed.

He pulled them on, left the room, and went down the corridor to the meeting hall where Dale had first taken them last night.

Zarkov and the android Martin were still seated by the huge windows that overlooked the city and, beyond it, a spectacular view of the cove and the waterfall. Dale was seated with Van d'Hoef and the young woman, Sandra Debonshire, at a small table.

When Flash came into the room, Van d'Hoef looked up, his face lighting up in a bright smile. "Good morning, Colonel Gordon," he said, and he jumped up and indicated a chair next to his. "Will you have something to eat?"

Flash came up to the table but then sat down across from the captain. "A cup of coffee, if you have such a thing," he said.

Van d'Hoef laughed and went to a narrow buffet behind the table. He poured a dark liquid from a container into a handleless cup. He came back and set it down on the table in front of Flash. "It's hot, dark, and wet. Not quite the same as real Earth coffee, but close."

Flash sipped the brew, which was very hot, and tasted surprisingly like coffee—perhaps even bet-

ter. But then he set his cup down and looked Van
d'Hoef directly in the eyes.

"There are a lot of questions I want answered
this morning. Questions, captain, that you avoided
last night."

Van d'Hoef, the smile gone from his face,
nodded slowly. "I'll answer everything."

"Who murdered your crew and passengers?"

Dale sat rigid in her chair, and out of the corner
of his eye Flash saw Zarkov and the android
Martin get up from their chairs and head toward
the table.

Van d'Hoef turned and glanced at the young
woman seated next to him. She had turned slightly
pale, and she lowered her head. "I did," she said
softly.

"Why?" Flash asked, a gentleness suddenly coming into his voice.

"I didn't want to," she said, her voice even lower. "God, I didn't want to, but it was the only
way."

"Perhaps I can better answer that question, colonel," the android Martin said.

Flash looked up as Zarkov and the android
pulled chairs around from another table and sat
down—Zarkov next to Dale, and Martin on the
other side of Van d'Hoef, next to the young woman.

For the first time Flash noticed that the android,
although humanlike in appearance, was slightly
different from the rest of them. Like the black robots from the data center, his arms and legs had
three joints each instead of just a single elbow or
knee, and his hands ended in a dozen thin, multi-

jointed digits. The effect was not one of great strength, but rather of obviously marvelous dexterity and agility.

His face was kind, however, his eyes a deep, rich blue, and his thick hair a silvery white. He glanced at the young woman and smiled almost sadly.

"If you'd rather not remain for this, why don't you leave, Sandra? You don't have to stay."

She looked up and shook her head. "It's all right," she said.

Martin looked at her for several seconds longer, but then seemed to sigh, and turned finally to look at Flash.

"Dr. Zarkov and I have been having quite a conversation this morning. He now understands much of what is happening here and why it has happened. But as I explained to him, Colonel Gordon, I wanted you all together to hear the entire story. It is a story that until the *Goodhope*'s crew arrived I had been waiting more than twenty thousand years to tell."

"You're twenty thousand years old," Flash said, stunned.

The android nodded. "I'm a bit older than that, but not quite as old as this city, although I was constructed shortly after the Citadel was completed."

"What about the thing we saw in the western sky last night?" Flash asked on impulse.

"That is the one thing I will not be able to explain for you. It was there before I was constructed. It is a legacy, if you will, of my creators. Beyond that I can tell you nothing about it other than the fact that the phenomenon occurs at totally unpredictable intervals. The last time it happened was nearly eighty of your Earth years ago. Before that it had been nearly a thousand years. I have only witnessed it a half a dozen times in my existence."

The android paused for a moment, cocked his head slightly, as if he were thinking about something that required his utmost concentration, and then looked up again. "We are digressing, and there is much to tell. Once I have finished my story, you and Dr. Zarkov and his lovely niece will have to make a decision. You will either remain here or return to Earth."

Flash sat forward, nearly spilling his coffee. "We can return? You have the means for us to return?"

Martin nodded. "Dr. Zarkov understands this. From his specifications, we can construct a deep space vessel exactly like your ship the *Intrepid*, and you will be shown a hyperpoint that would bring you to the rim of your Federation. From that point the memory you have of this place would be erased from your minds. You would not be able to find us for centuries."

"And our other choice, if we are to have a decision?" Flash asked.

"To remain here and help us."

Flash slowly sat back in his chair.

"I will only give you enough information for you to make your decision this morning. Should you elect to remain, we have devices that are capable of imprinting on your brains the entire history of the Citadel, along with as much of our technology as you can absorb."

There was a long silence between them, until

finally Zarkov spoke up. "Proceed, Martin," he said, and the android in a very humanlike gesture folded his hands together in front of him on the table.

The lights in the room dimmed, the large windows overlooking the bright, sunny day went opaque, and a holographic projection of a nude man and woman, very similar in appearance to Martin, appeared at the center of the table.

"My creators," the android said.

The figures were beautiful, their bodies lithe and well tanned, and both with shimmering silver hair. But as Martin began to talk, the holographic images at the center of the table began to shift and change into views of vast cities, huge machinery, space vessels, and even terrible battles.

"As long as one billion years ago, there arose in this galaxy two separate and quite distinctly different civilizations. Until quite late in my creators' development the two civilizations were unaware of each other's existence.

"A galactic empire flourished in our part of the galaxy, spreading out from the core stars in every direction. There was a vast empire council of leaders, there was peace for many thousands of years, there was fabulous trade between worlds of hundreds of thousands of different cultures, all unified under one precept . . . that of peace and good fellowship toward all sentient creatures."

The holographic image of the great city, much larger and more beautiful than the city they were in at the present, appeared at the center of the table.

"The central city—Centrus, as closely as I can translate—where government, literature, art, and fine music flourished, and where the end finally came."

Martin was an android, a machine, but he was more sophisticated than any Guardian computer Flash had ever seen. And now he seemed almost sad. As if he had personally been a part of the times he was talking about, and he was looking back on them with nostalgia.

"That was nearly one hundred thousand years ago. At the height of our empire the other civilization was discovered." There was suddenly a bitterness in his voice. "It began with contact between exploration vessels well beyond our farthermost rim system. The crew of our ship was murdered, their vessel and its records and technology studied. Within a dozen years the first attacks came on our rim systems, which were virtually defenseless against the onslaught."

The holograph changed into a three-dimensional map of the Milky Way galaxy.

"Your system is located with us in one of the spiral arms of our galaxy, which is one hundred thousand light-years across. My creators' empire flourished near the center of the galaxy. The other civilization is in the opposite rim. With 30 billion stars in the galaxy, we occupied systems around more than 10 million stars."

Flash and Zarkov were flabbergasted, and it showed in their expressions. Martin smiled.

"Yes," he said softly. "Ours was a vast empire, vast far beyond your comprehension at this moment. But it had nearly one billion years to develop before the others came."

"There was a great war," Flash said, awed.

"A war beyond belief," Martin said. "A war that lasted without peace for more than eighty thousand years. A war so colossal it literally drained the resources of an entire galaxy. The ultimate insanity of supposedly rational beings."

"And your people won?" Flash asked.

Martin shook his head. "No one won. Everyone lost. Our empire decayed as did, we surmise, the other empire. But after so many tens of thousands of years, the idea of war was so totally ingrained in my creators' genetic makeup that the very concept of peace nearly became impossible to comprehend. But by then our empire was in its death throes. Contact with all but a handful of core worlds was irrevocably lost. Piracy was rampant. Violence was everywhere. Assassination, riot, and anarchy all reigned supreme. Later we learned that a similar breakdown occurred in the other empire. But it was a small consolation. The most fabulous creation of all time had been destroyed."

Flash's coffee sat untouched, and he hardly dared breathe as he tried without success to envision the colossal concepts the android was trying to make him see. Civilizations one billion years old. Wars that lasted eighty thousand years, involving millions of planetary systems. It was too much to comprehend.

"A group of my creators, only several hundred thousand of them, fled Centrus some twenty thousand years ago, finally coming to this planet. Here they were beyond even the rim of the original empire, and completely across the galaxy from the remnants of the other civilization. Here was peace. And it was here they built what they called Citadel, the repository for all the surviving knowledge of our empire. All the technology that they could bring with them, all the art, the music, everything that goes to make up a civilization, was brought here."

"In the computer we saw?" Zarkov asked. He too was awed, his voice barely audible.

"You saw only the planetary control systems, nothing more," Martin said. "The *entire* planet was hollowed out, and in its place a computer constructed. The entire planet is the repository for the empire's knowledge. When it was completed I was built."

"This city?" Dale asked.

"Was where the last of the empire's citizens lived, worked, and departed."

"What happened to them?" Zarkov asked.

"Soon after their work was completed scientists left aboard a gigantic vessel constructed from the material taken from the planet's core. Their destination was the galaxy Andromeda, as you call it, nearly one million light-years distant."

"Why did they all leave after settling and building on this planet? And why did they build this in the first place?" Zarkov asked.

"They built this so that the knowledge of the empire would not be forever lost. But they *all* didn't leave at first. Only the scientists left in the huge ship. And they did so because they saw that someday there could be a repeat of what happened with the first empire. They wanted to travel to another galaxy in the hope of either finding peace for their kind at long last, or at the very least of finding a civilization that they could save from a similar fate."

"And those who remained?" Zarkov continued to question the android.

"They finally left too. In small scout ships, scattering their seed in all directions." Again the look of sadness crossed the machine's features. "But they were ill-equipped to deal with raw, new worlds." He looked into Zarkov's eyes. "One ship, from what I understand, landed on your planet, something under 10 thousand of your years ago. We have heard nothing from them in all this time. It is assumed they either died in the attempt to land, or died shortly thereafter."

"There are stories," Zarkov said, "ancient stories of lost civilizations, of ships from the stars. No one has really believed them . . ." He trailed off.

Martin smiled almost indulgently. "Which brings us to the present."

"Which brings us to the *Goodhope*," Flash corrected, sitting forward.

Martin looked at him. "Before I explain that, I must explain one other thing."

Flash said nothing, waiting for the android to continue.

"The other civilization. The one that brought war to this galaxy, has had a similar development. When its empire began to break up, its scientists also constructed a repository of knowledge much similar to this one. We have sent probes out as recently as two thousand years ago. Across the galaxy is Citadel II. A planetwide computer just like this one preserves all that civilization's knowledge, including its desire for war."

"We are a long way from expanding outward to that civilization," Flash said.

"Until your return here aboard the *Goodhope*, I would have agreed with you. But that is not the case. We have evidently been discovered. When we detected the *Goodhope* coming with you out of hyper space, we also detected a drive unit not of our design. It is of the design of the other civilization. They have discovered us, as well as the fact that we have the help of the *Goodhope*'s crew."

Zarkov paled. "My God," he whispered.

Martin sat forward, ignoring Zarkov for the moment, concentrating on Flash. "You are a military man, Colonel Gordon. You understand war and fighting, but you must understand something else. I am nothing more than a machine—a sophisticated machine by your standards, but still nothing more than a machine. As primitive as your people are, compared to what my creators were at the height of their empire, you have something I do not have. That is intuition. Intuitive intelligence. No machine has been built that can match that. No machine has the vitality and energy of even an uncivilized sentient being."

Through the discussion Flash had begun to build up a grudging respect for Martin, and he found it difficult now to accept the fact that he was nothing more than a machine. A robot. "But machines do make war."

"No," Martin said sadly. "And that brings us to our present difficulty."

"The other Citadel planet," Flash said.

"Yes," Martin said, and he stood up. The holographic projection shimmered and died, the lights came back on, and the window again became translucent to admit the sun.

"The creators, when they built the Citadel, infused within its being two directives," the android said. He crossed the room and looked out the window down at the city.

Flash and the others got up and took seats near the machine. When they were settled, Martin continued.

"The first was to watch for the emergence of new civilizations. They were aware of other developing life forms throughout the galaxy." He turned away from the window. "And the second directive was to watch for any signs that the other empire was returning."

"Both conditions have been found," Zarkov prompted after a moment of silence, and Martin nodded. "What was your prime directive in that case?"

"There was a prime directive for each circumstance. We were to avoid contact with any emergent civilization until it was advanced enough to understand and not misuse what knowledge is contained here. And we were to resist with the *minimum* necessary force any attempt by the second empire to gain control of the galaxy. But I simply cannot meet those conditions alone.

"It was believed by my creators that the technicians and others who remained behind would stay here, populate this planet, and use the computer system to meet those directives. They were a peace loving people, or wanted to be, and they had the intuitive genius I lack. But they left and never returned."

"You became aware of the *Goodhope,* our first intersteller effort, and you went after her for her crew?" Zarkov asked.

Martin looked down at Sandra Debonshire, and

nodded. "I thought that the crew of the *Goodhope* could answer two problems. The first was my need for sentient beings to take over here. And the second was to push back any attempt by your race to come this far. Your people, on the whole, are not ready for the Citadel."

"How did you accomplish that?" Zarkov asked.

"My scout machines, which are out at all times looking for traces of the other civilization, as well as for the rise of new sentient races, detected the *Goodhope* and reported back. I went out to the ship, brought the entire crew and passenger complement back here, and explained everything to them as I have explained it to you. They all agreed to help. It was a challenge. It was a matter of survival."

"I'd like to say it was our sense of duty to the safety of the galaxy," Van d'Hoef interjected wryly. "But it was probably more like selfishness that made us stay. We were offered practical immortality. And power. So we accepted."

"So you accepted," Flash said. "But why did you go back and kill yourselves? Why did you set the *Goodhope* adrift? You knew that sooner or later someone would find the ship. Find your bodies. Why didn't you just bring the ship here? Or destroy it?"

"Because the search would have continued for us," Van d'Hoef said.

"We gave it up forty years ago," Flash said bitterly. "The *Goodhope* was listed as lost."

"Sooner or later the search would have been taken up again," Martin said. "From what I have learned of the crew of the *Goodhope*, your race has the characteristic of not easily giving up any project. You would have come looking for the *Goodhope*. Sooner or later your people would have found this planet."

"I don't buy that argument," Flash said, and he got up from his chair to pace the floor in front of the window. The day was bright and beautiful, the rainbow over the waterfall in the distance like some picture out of an ancient fairy tale.

"I'm afraid I convinced them of the logic of it," Sandra Debonshire said. "I am a psychologist. I was certain that a search would be mounted unless the *Goodhope* returned with us dead."

"So you went back to a point in time earlier than your departure, and killed the crew and passengers . . . including yourself." Flash said incredulously.

The young woman nodded. "At the last minute I could not kill myself . . . at least, not in the way I had killed the others. So I pulled my own body out of the cryo unit and pushed it out an airlock."

Dale stifled a gasp.

"If and when the ship was finally discovered, it would have seemed as if I had gone berserk, killed everyone on board, and jumped ship," she said.

"And now what?" Flash asked, completely disgusted.

"Citadel II's scouts unfortunately discovered the *Goodhope* before your people did. They figured out what we had done, installed a hyper drive generator aboard, and sent your vessel back . . . into your Federation shipping lanes, from what Dr. Zarkov tells me," Martin said.

"Why?" Flash asked sharply. He wanted to hit something.

"They want war," Martin said. "They want your Federation to mount an attack on them. They exist for the very idea of war. Our scientists built this Citadel. Their war strategists built their Citadel planet. By sending the *Goodhope* back to your Federation with the bodies aboard, they hoped to provoke a violent reaction. The hyper drive unit was programmed to return here. Your Federation, armed with the knowledge of this Citadel world, would make a formidable force. Exactly what the others want."

"And it took nearly one billion years of civilization for your makers to develop that philosophy?" Flash shouted.

Martin came over to where Flash stood by the window, placed a hand on his shoulder, and smiled. "You have the qualities my creators wanted most to instill into this galaxy. Qualities that their civilization once had but lost. You understand war and violence, but you hate it, and all that it stands for. If you will agree to help, I know there will be peace for all of us. Peace everlasting, and a second empire that could someday reach out to touch the empire that may already be abuilding with my creators in the Andromeda galaxy."

Flash looked into the android robot's eyes, but was seeing a picture of a beautiful young woman lying dead, beaten to death. And then he was seeing the 157 men and women of the *Goodhope,* their throats slit, their bodies decaying. And a wave of revulsion swept through his body.

Violence, the android had been talking about. But violence on a scale so vast that it was nearly impossible to accept.

And yet not only was he being asked to accept the possibility that such violence could exist, he was also being asked to accept the fact that it could very well happen again, and very soon. And, he was being asked to help.

Could he refuse?

He turned to look at Dale, who sat on the edge of her chair anxiously watching him. Beside her, Zarkov had drawn inward and was struggling with his own thoughts.

Could he refuse?

His eyes fell on Sandra Debonshire, who had gone through more than any of them could envision. And Captain Van d'Hoef, who had suggested, or at least condoned, the crime.

Could he refuse?

And then he turned to look at Martin beside him, an android robot, who seemed more humane than any person he had ever met. And he hung his head.

"How can I refuse?" he said softly.

Martin's grip tightened on his shoulder. "You can't," the android said. "You can't."

No, he could not, he thought. Even though it meant they would have to remain here, out of contact with Earth, out of contact with their lives back home, for many months, perhaps even years.

He looked again at Dale and Dr. Zarkov, and they both nodded. They had made their choices. Then he looked up at Martin. "We'll help," he said. "However long it takes, we'll help."